I0545174

Cryptic Blend

A PARAMOUR BAY MYSTERY
BOOK SEVEN

KENNEDY LAYNE

CRYPTIC BLEND

DEDICATION

Jeffrey—Nothing cryptic about it! I love you…

Cole—Your freshman year of college is now complete, and you're already beginning a career that you love. We are so proud of you!

Ghosts, goblins, and ghouls go bump in the night in the latest installment of the Paramour Bay Mysteries by USA Today Bestselling Author Kennedy Layne...

The residents in the small coastal town of Paramour Bay are sorting through their unwanted belongings and setting up card tables in their driveways in order to get ready for their annual community garage sale.

Raven Marigold hasn't lived in town long enough to contribute to the garage sale, but she sure is ready to find some basement bargains. Armed with a small reserve of cash and a large tote for her treasure trove, she wasn't prepared for her familiar to make a shocking discovery of an authentic sapphire pendant. You see, the disturbing part of such a find was that the pendant belonged to a resident...one who'd been buried with it.

A haunted cemetery, an empty crypt, and a rather curious raccoon are all cryptic clues in another magical mystery that will leave you gasping for breath until the very last page!

Chapter One

THE WARMTH OF the sun had hit that perfect temperature. You know the moment, the one right at the end of the day before evening truly set in. It was such a magical time, and it made me wish that I was sitting in my patio chair overlooking the water of the bay.

As it stood, I was currently browsing through the various jumbled tables at the annual garage sale. There were rows upon rows of long forgotten but once cherished knickknacks, board games with most of the pegs still present, and puzzles missing that one jigsaw piece that would haunt a person for days.

Granted, it was going on six o'clock in the early evening. Most of the gently used items had been picked over more than once, but it was still fun to get into the spirit of cleaning house. I hadn't lived in Paramour Bay long enough to accumulate excess material treasures that I no longer needed nor wanted. It was one of the reasons I'd come armed with a small stack of ones and a tote for any pearl I could snatch away from the jaws of destiny.

The charming neighborhoods of our community were busy with neighbors and families milling about in the small collection of driveways of appealing two-story Cape Cod-style homes common to the environs of coastal Connecticut. They each came with their perfectly manicured lawns. I swear, it made me wonder who made up the committee that graded the effort each homeowner put in as they clipped each blade of grass with a pair of sewing scissors.

The weather this month had been absolutely fabulous, and the sweet fragrance of fresh cut grass hung in the air along with the sweet blooms of the lilac bushes. The birds were chirping high up in the trees, thankful for the abundant bounty in their native breeding grounds after the now forgotten spring migration north. The bumblebees were busy pollinating nature's bouquet of flowers, and sales at the shop were higher than ever before.

My Nan would be ecstatic at the amount of revenue *Tea, Leaves, & Eves* had drawn in this quarter, and we still had a month left on the books. It seemed my small contribution of coffee inventory to the business had been realized, and the shop was a success beyond my wildest dreams.

This quaint coastal town of Paramour Bay, Connecticut had become a home to me only this past October after the unexpected death of my grandmother, Rosemary Lattice Marigold. We hadn't been very close before her passing, and I very much regretted that my mother had done her best to keep us apart during the most influential years of my life.

Technically, I hadn't spoken to my Nan for close to twelve years prior to her attorney's call on my cell phone to inform me of her passing and my inheritance. Even though I hadn't known it at the time, it was a phone call that had changed the course of my life…in many, many ways.

"You have got to see this cute wicker basket that Dee Fairuza has for only three dollars," Heidi Connolly exclaimed, sidling up to me with a tote full of magnificent items herself. My best friend had gotten a head start on me earlier this afternoon, but my shop's hours were from eight to five o'clock, six days a week, and my part-time employee had the day off. "The weave is actually varnished in a deep cherry color with a red ribbon accent. Can you believe the coincidence? Oh, and it would go perfect in my new office on the credenza behind my desk."

Heidi and I had very different tastes, but I'd kept that in mind when I'd created the hex bag for her as a congratulatory office gift—which just so happened to be made with black rustic burlap and a red bow accent. I'd put the finishing touches on the magical gift last night. Let's just say I'm not quite the expert at casting spells, so generating a magical hex bag that warded off evil spirits had taken me a few weeks to perfect. The silver lining in the rough weave of the burlap was that nothing bad had occurred after the final binding spell.

"Go snag it up before someone else absconds with your heart's delight," I advised, pointing toward a whimsical scarf that had caught my eye. It made me think of Paris in the spring. The emerald green hues were juxtaposed by the fascinating blues, and the colors would go perfectly with my peacock earrings. I didn't want to chance someone else buying it before I could hand over my dollar bill. "I want to buy that scarf from Karen. I can't believe she's selling it."

"Okay, but meet me over at Dee's table the moment you're done." Heidi hoisted up her heavy tote laden with her newfound treasures over her shoulder, her blonde curls getting stuck underneath. She didn't seem to mind, though, as she began to march onward in search of more elusive booty. She made sure to get in the last word over her shoulder. "I want your thoughts on a cut crystal bowl that I might buy for my desk. I remembered Beetle said he always kept mints and hard candy on hand for his customers. I'm thinking I should do the same."

Beetle was the former accountant in town, and the one who'd sold his small firm and his Rolodex of dedicated customers to Heidi. It was her dream come true to own her own financial advisor and accounting business, and our lives had finally gotten on a track where there was only a bright clear path ahead.

Speaking of Beetle, though, he just so happened to be my new part-time employee at the tea shop. He'd still wanted to keep his beak wet, whatever that meant. He was eager for something to do during his retirement so that he wasn't sitting idle, but he sure wasn't the finest student of the retail side of things. He was a creature of habit after all those years calculating taxes, so not necessarily the best salesclerk. On the bright side, the shop's books have never been more balanced than they were today.

"Hi, Karen," I called out as I began to walk up her driveway. She had initially set up four tables, but she'd consolidated what she had left onto two smaller ones as she sold off her wares. It was a good bet that by the time seven o'clock rolled around, she'd only have a few items left to store in a box in her garage for next year or she might just give them to charity. "Has today been a success?"

"Oh, yes," Karen exclaimed, leaning forward on her chair so that she could rest her elbows on the table next to a small grey tea box where she was no doubt keeping her earnings from today's sales. Empty tea boxes were just like cigar boxes in the end. They tended to accumulate keepsakes after they were emptied of their original contents. "Heidi stopped by earlier and bought some knickknacks for her new house. I bet you're thrilled that she's finally moved to town."

"I am," I replied with a genuine smile. "Having her here all the time makes Paramour Bay feel a lot more like home to me. How's Otis doing with his arthritis?"

I picked up the scarf, noticing the price tag read one dollar as expected. It was too bad that Karen wasn't selling more scarves like this one or else I would have bought at least ten of them. My taste in clothes aired on the side of whimsical, with flowy sleeves and peacock skirts that twirled around my ankles rather than above my knees like most women my age.

I guess one could say with my long black hair, emerald green eyes, and prominent cheekbones that I resembled a witch. The title no longer bothered me, and I had come to embrace the Marigold lineage with enthusiasm. There was something cathartic about giving back to the community in a way that almost no one else knew about outside of the magical realm.

Well, with the exception of Heidi, of course.

It had been beyond my ability to keep her in the dark about the most significant discovery of my new life. After all, she was my best friend whom I confided everything to, and keeping secrets from her just wasn't in the cards. Of course, I'd broken a sacred coven rule by doing so, but I couldn't see what all the fuss was about considering the Marigold family had been excommunicated from the coven, anyway.

The banishment had happened many, many years ago for consorting with a male human against the explicit demands of the governing council. Expulsion and cutting ties with the coven had been Nan's punishment, and she'd chosen Paramour Bay as her home until it had been her time to cross into the afterlife.

"I swear, that tea blend you sell my husband every week must be magic. Being the sheriff for so many years took a toll on his knees, that's for sure. He's actually golfing today, if you can believe that. Nothing like retirement and a healthy outlook to get one out of the house on such a beautiful day. He left the house by four-thirty this morning, bent on catching a few prime bluegill before his afternoon tee time." Karen took the dollar bill that I'd fished out of my wallet before pointing up the street with a concerned expression. "Isn't that your rescue cat? It was so sweet of you to take in such a disheveled-looking thing, and he's become so loyal to you in return. I can only imagine what your vet bills must be every month, but the love of a rescue animal is unlike any other, isn't it? Why, our Dolly is going to be fourteen years old this summer, and she's the light of our lives."

I took no offense to the fact that everyone thought my familiar, Leo, had to be a rescue cat. His appearance did leave a lot to be desired, what with his bulging left eye and crooked whiskers. I shouldn't leave out that his tail resembled a hanger that someone had used as a makeshift antenna. He was also carrying a bit of too much weight for the size of his munchkin legs, and there were tufts of hair sticking out at various odd angles.

Technically, Leo had belonged to my Nan.

You see, Nan had broken another coven rule by dabbling in dark magic. Her intentions had been good, though. As a matter of fact, her using a necromancy spell to keep Leo from crossing over to the other realm had been done in the name of love. Not that there was just one plane of existence to move on to, because in reality there were a vast amount more.

Sorry.

Sometimes I get distracted with all the new things I've come to discover within the supernatural realm.

Getting back to where we were...

Nan had wanted Leo left on this plane of existence so that I had someone to guide me through this new life I'd been granted. Witchcraft wasn't an easy craft to learn, you know. I definitely needed the extra help.

Mind you, I was referring to white magic. I couldn't even

imagine dabbling in black magic like Nan had done on a few occasions, especially when doing so resulted in unwanted consequences for everyone involved. It was the major reason for Leo's disheveled appearance. Then there was the other result of dark magic—his short-term memory loss.

Short-term might be a bit too generous, but that saga was a story for another time.

Anyway, I hadn't known the Marigold women were witches until last October, Halloween to be exact, when I'd moved my entire life here to Paramour Bay. Trust me, I'd thought I was going certifiably insane the first time I'd heard Leo speak as if he were a person. I had been one phone call away from having Heidi whisk me off to the looney bin, but Leo had quickly caught me up on the life of a Marigold that I had been meant to live.

Raven, Raven.

Speak of the devil.

Have you seen Skippy? His evil band of ninja squirrels chucked some acorns at my head. I could have gotten a concussion if their aim wasn't so bad. They've taken things too far this time, and it's going to mean their demise. This town is only big enough for one master, and I want it back. They have no idea the resources I have at my disposal.

I tucked my new scarf into my tote bag before kneeling down and stroking Leo's back. He must be really worked up over his ongoing battle with the neighborhood squirrels, because he was usually careful about talking to me in front of the other residents. Not that they could hear him, and he usually disappeared when the going got tough.

Who was I kidding?

Leo could have cared less who heard his raspy meow. Plus,

he would have thought it a bonus had I flubbed up and been made to look foolish talking to him as if he were my only friend in the world. He'd been laughing over his comment about me becoming the old hag living on the edge of town with only her cat for company.

"Leo, what are you doing so far away from the tea shop?" I murmured, wanting Karen to believe that I had things under control. "Did you miss me?"

Cut the sappy stuff, Raven. I'm serious. That squirrel has got to go. Have you seen Skippy or not? I've been hunting him all day, but he's been one step ahead of me the entire afternoon. He and his minions have gotten smarter, and they are just one acorn away from world domination.

I hadn't seen the particular squirrel that Leo was referring to, but then again, I'd been working much of the day inside my shop. Skippy was easier to spot than the other squirrels due to the white patch of fur he had on the side of his right leg. I'm pretty sure it was a war wound from last year's epic battle.

Fine. I'll just have to wait until tomorrow morning to restart my hunt, but I'm not getting up before sunrise. It's unseemly to be dragging my old rear out of bed before the sun comes up. Besides, it's Friday night. I plan to smoke my catnip pipe in celebration that your latest spell didn't kill anyone off. That reminds me, did my monthly supply of premium organic catnip arrive at the shop today? I'm expecting a delivery from Honduras. I really don't like it when you give Beetle the day off. I didn't get my special edible treat this morning. It's beyond cruel.

"I think Leo has actually lost a pound or two," Karen said after having peered over the table to look down at him. "This is a safe neighborhood, Raven. Everyone knows Leo, and he's a smart enough cat to stick to the yards. I think his daily walks are getting him in shape."

One insult, and one compliment. How am I supposed to react to that kind of ambiguity, Raven? Never mind, don't answer that. I'll meet you at home away from the peasants. All this social mingling is likely to make my tufts fall out.

Only Leo would take the compliment of losing weight as an insult. He probably thought I was starving him to death. Heidi had been telling him that he had the frame of a Greek god, just as any self-respecting tomcat should. She was very good for his ego.

"Leo does like to roam the neighborhoods from time to time," I replied with a smile. "I should get going. Heidi wants me to take a look at a basket that Dee is selling."

"Are you sure you don't want the bracelet that I bought to go along with that scarf?" Karen pointed toward the end of the table, where a small basket of costume jewelry sat by its lonesome. "It's nothing fancy, but I just don't like the feel of anything jangling on my wrists anymore. It gives me the heebie-jeebies nowadays. It's amazing how our tastes change the older we get, isn't it?"

Considering that I was only thirty years old, I'm pretty sure that was a rhetorical question. I personally loved bracelets, and the more they jingled the better in my mind. The sign hanging on the basket read fifty cents apiece, and that was one bargain I couldn't pass up. Heidi would wait for me, plus she would completely understand since my delay was due to my costume jewelry fetish.

Can you manage a second to look up in that tree for me? I can't quite see that squirrel's side, and the coastal breeze is going in the opposite direction. It might very well be Skippy, hiding there in plain sight.

I did as Leo asked, knowing he wouldn't head home until I verified whether or not it was Skippy in the tree. A quick glance revealed that it was just another random squirrel ninja, and not Leo's diabolical nemesis…Skippy the squirrel.

It didn't take me long to dive into the various bracelets, necklaces, and rings. I was definitely going to have to purchase the matching bracelet, because the emerald green hue was absolutely my favorite color with the occasional blue sapphire accent. I was just about to turn away after having chosen three bracelets and one necklace to make this an easy transaction when a specific ring caught my attention.

I slid the piece of jewelry onto my right ring finger and held up my hand to get a better look, unsure if it suited my taste. For being just costume jewelry, the gem certainly looked like a real sapphire. Of course, these days with lab-grown stones, one could hardly tell the real thing from plastic. My mother loved real sapphires, so I could usually tell the difference between those and the fake lab-created jewels.

This time?

Not so much.

Uh, Raven.

I slowly lowered my hand, having heard that tone a bit too much in the past seven months. It was usually when Leo was about to tell me a spell I'd cast hadn't gone quite as planned or when there was a ghost drifting about the area.

Now that I think about it, the palm of my hand had become a bit warm.

Any time my palm harnessed a bit of energy from the earth, it was usually a telltale sign when danger was near. I'd chalked up this time to the lone ray of sunshine I'd purposefully held my hand into in order to get a better look at the fake sapphire, but I was no longer interested in the accessory. I began to work the ring off my finger in preparation that I'd need to leave the garage sale sooner than anticipated.

Had Leo seen another ghost?

Was someone walking nearby who didn't have good intentions?

You might want to take that particular ring off your finger a bit faster than that.

The ring?

Leo was worried about costume jewelry?

Costume jewelry? My dear Raven, I will have you know that ring is very much the real deal. One of a kind, as a matter of fact, and worth tens of thousands of dollars. It belonged to one Caroline Abigail Whitley, the wife of an original founder of Paramour Bay.

Leo's memory certainly wasn't failing him now.

I've heard of people making astonishing finds at garage sales, but my luck didn't usually run in that direction. Of course, those individuals were usually professionals who had an eye for antiques or relics from generations past. I'd likened myself to the casual customer on the "Antiques Roadshow" who ended up owning a long-lost Renoir painting.

Karen was asking fifty cents for a ring that was probably worth tens of thousands and thousands of dollars. I could make the choice of paying her and walking away from the table with an absolute steal, but that's exactly what it would be—stealing.

You have this situation all wrong, Raven.

"Karen, are you sure you want to sell this ring?" I asked, carrying my purchases in one hand while hold the ring up with my other. "I think this sapphire is real."

It wasn't like I could tell her that I knew the ring belonged to Caroline Abigail Whitley.

I'd definitely bring up that itsy-bitsy detail if I were you.

"I don't think I've seen that particular piece of jewelry before," Karen asked with a quizzical frown. She took the ring and inspected it before handing it back to me. "It must have been mixed in with some of the other costume pieces I had in a shoebox. Trust me, Raven, this is not a genuine sapphire. The only real piece of jewelry I own is my wedding band."

I was not going to bring up the fact that this ring belonged to a dead woman. Doing so would mean that I'd have to fabricate some complicated excuse that would only end up getting me in trouble.

I was a terrible liar, just ask Heidi.

Horrible was more accurate.

I couldn't believe Leo would suggest I attempt such a feat over something so trivial.

Trivial? You're holding a dead woman's ring, Raven. That's not trivial, and we may very well have a major problem on our hands.

"I'll tell you what," I replied to Karen with a fantastic compromise in mind. "I'll buy the ring, but I'll return it to you if I find out that it's the real deal."

As for Leo being uncomfortable with me owning an item of someone deceased, then he wasn't thinking clearly. Nan had not only left me the tea shop, but I'd also inherited her eerie cottage on the edge of town that came with its very own wax golem.

You're missing the oh-so-relevant point, dear Raven.

Karen agreed with a smile that told me she didn't believe for one second that the sapphire ring was real, which made me wonder if Leo's memory issues hadn't come into play. He did tend to get a few facts mixed up from time to time. I set the jewelry down so that I could reach into my tote once more for my wallet.

I hate to break it to you so indelicately, Raven, but you're not going to be able to buy yourself out of this snafu. Just when I think you can't top your last spell glitch, you up your game. I don't know whether to be proud of you or beg your grandmother's spirit for forgiveness.

Snafu?

Glitch?

I'd cast only one major spell this past week, and that had been Heidi's gift for finally being able to move into her newly renovated office. The hex bag had been crafted to ward off evil spirits. Leo wasn't saying…

Oh yes, I am saying. That ring does *belong to Caroline Abigail Whitley, but there's a catch you seem bent on not hearing. You see, that enormous and very expensive sapphire ring was her prized possession, and it just so happens that it was buried with her inside the family crypt when she went to the grave.*

My stomach bottomed out and my skin became clammy as I tried to open my wallet. Another spell gone wrong, this time involving malevolent spirits? There was no way that I could leave the ring behind now, especially when I was going to have to find a way to return it to its rightful owner.

I suddenly find myself in need of my pipe, Raven. You have the distinct ability to drive that need home. Aren't I the special one, indeed?

Chapter Two

"I CAN'T WEAR this thing." Heidi took off the black beanie she'd slid over her blonde curls and tossed it down on the couch. "It's too warm outside. Besides, I'd look ridiculous drowning in my own sweat, and then we'd have to come up with a doozy of an excuse as to why we're all creeping around the cemetery looking like a bunch of grave robbers. Don't you have a dark baseball cap or something more fashionable?"

We'd come back to the cottage almost immediately after Leo's bombshell landed with quite the explosion. I'd caught Heidi up as quickly as possible on the latest disaster, but we'd had no choice but to first swing by Heidi's new office to grab the botched hex bag.

I'd wanted to break the spell I'd cast in good faith, but Leo had been uncertain of doing such a reversal for fear that whatever I'd done would become permanent. He also mentioned that he wasn't sure if the energy from the ring might interfere with any spell I'd cast, and I had to agree with that assumption. It was always better to be safe than sorry. As for the hex bag, its current location was in a hidden drawer within my coffee table. It couldn't be safer.

Tell my beloved Heidi that it's not going to matter what she wears tonight, and that being caught by a human will be the least of our worries. If we are dealing with the spirit of Caroline Abigail

Whitley, we're probably all going to die horrible deaths. Let me at least get in a few puffs of my organic catnip before I meet Nan for a snack at the cafeteria later. Do you suppose the afterlife has fresh sushi at the self-service counter after hours?

I wasn't going to tell Heidi anything of what Leo had rambled on about. He and I had dealt with ghosts before, and the encounter hadn't been all that bad. As a matter of fact, the spirit of Mazie Rose Young had gone back to the afterlife a very happy camper with her fairy familiar in tow. From what she'd told us, we'd gained a well-regarded reputation as amateur sleuths of the supernatural realm. And just for the record, I highly doubted that they served sushi of any sort, even during regular business hours in the afterlife.

My dear Mazie was an absolute teetotaler with a proper sense of humor and a kind soul, unlike that trickster of a fairy who delighted in marking ruggedly handsome cats with her annoying glitter dust lipstick. I still can't get this mark off my fur...not that it will matter. As I said, we're doomed to die horrible deaths.

"I might have a baseball cap up in the loft, tucked in behind my scarves somewhere." I semi-recalled when I bought a midnight blue New York Yankees ball cap on a windy day when I lived in the city. I finally finished tying my black laces on my matching running shoe that were currently on my feet, thinking over what Leo had said about Mazie and our current problem. "Leo, are you insinuating that Mrs. Whitley wasn't in the good graces of her neighbors when she was alive? How would you know that when you weren't even alive back then? Wait. Were you? Alive back then, I mean?"

I guess I hadn't thought to ask Leo how old he was, just assuming he'd come into existence sometime during Nan's tenure as a novice witch. I'd been meaning to finish going through the family history notes that were tucked away in the boxes upstairs, but life and issues with my spells kept getting in the way.

Let's just say I've been around for longer than was probably necessary, but it can take many centuries for a familiar to be joined with his or her proper caster. Until we are called upon by our magical match, we usually just stay near the coven of our origin. In doing so, I was quite familiar—oh, look at what I did there. No pun intended, of course, though I do believe this organic catnip does make me a bit wittier. Anyway, I was very well-acquainted with the surrounding areas. In order to respect the dead, I will only say that Mrs. Caroline Abigail Whitney was known for being quite challenging back in her day. Back to this sushi business. I have it on good order that the sushi is quite extraordinary in the afterlife. Their spring rolls are to die for...oops. I did it again. These puns just seem to come out of nowhere, Raven.

"Are you absolutely sure Mrs. Whitley was buried with her sapphire ring and that this is the same one she took to her grave?" I asked for the hundredth time, and for many more reasons than I could possibly articulate. As I'd mentioned before, Leo's memory went on the fritz a bit too often than either of us cared to admit. "I'd hate to think we're sneaking into a graveyard after dark for absolutely no reason."

"How does this look?" Heidi asked after having used the spiral staircase that led to the bedroom loft. She was walking toward me with my Yankees baseball cap pulled down low on her forehead. She'd borrowed one of my long-sleeved black t-shirts and skin-tight yoga pants in the same inky black. "Do I look ready to break into a crypt or am I just that good?"

"Stop saying that," I muttered with agitation, unhappier with myself now that I'd gotten us into another pickle. "We're not breaking into a crypt. We're simply visiting the cemetery to see if the crypt has been disturbed in any fashion or if Leo's memory from so long ago is just a bit fuzzy."

Please, please let the problem lie with Leo's memory.

Are you actually praying to the Sweet Angel of Mercy? I will have you know that I always fess up when my memory goes into the toilet. This is not one of those times, so I suggest pulling up your bootstraps, missy. We're going ghost hunting!

I practically collapsed back into the overstuffed chair in frustration, uncomfortable with these dark clothes that were stifling my free spirit at the same time it destroyed my sense of fashion. I hardly ever wore clothes like these, of course, but Heidi could make the grave robber style look chic.

Moreover, I was going to need to blend in with the shadows so as not to be seen entering any crypt. We had no legitimate reason to be visiting the town's local cemetery at ten o'clock on a Friday night.

"Raven, I've seen a lot of unexplainable things happen since you told me you were a witch." Heidi sat on the couch and rested her elbows on her knees so she could lean forward in her attempt to ease my fears. Her blue eyes softened when she smiled in reassurance. "I can only assume that learning something as difficult as witchcraft is as complicated as learning how to perform brain surgery on a running horse. It takes many, many years to become the best in one's field. No one expects you to be perfect right out of the gate. The one thing you've been able to accomplish that those surgeons will never have the chance to do is the ability to fix your mistakes, right? There hasn't been one spell cast that didn't eventually contribute to getting the incantation right in the end. So, don't beat yourself up. Besides, Jack is at some training course in North Carolina, and I'm bored out of my mind. Before planning our nightly excursion, my Friday night consisted of me binge watching 'Sabrina the Teenage Witch' to see if her life was anything like yours. I'll get back to you on that later."

I truly didn't believe that anything else could make this night worse, but Heidi just had to mention that oaf of a detective who hovers over her like locusts over a ripe fruit orchard.

Heidi was currently dating Detective Jack Swanson, and he was honestly the longest running candidate for what you might call a long-term relationship when it came to Heidi. Leo took exception, of course. He didn't think anyone was good enough for his lovely Heidi, but Jack was kind, compassionate, and supportive of her move from New York City to an out-of-the-way coastal Connecticut town. One that happened to be quieter and safer than any borough in the big city.

It wasn't that New York was any more dangerous than any other metropolis. Heck, I'd been born and raised there myself. But statistically wise, Paramour Bay had the lowest crime rates of any other town in the country, with jaywalking usually being the worst misconduct during any given afternoon.

Are you the one with the memory problem? I distinctly recall there being a murderous clown running around this town only last month. Oh, and let's not forget about the tax guy who bit the dust just before Christmas. Here. Take a hit off my pipe. Catnip makes everything seem so much better.

I wasn't going to let Leo ruin this supportive moment. I'd needed it desperately, and tonight's scavenger hunt no longer seemed that bad given the other possibilities. Besides, Heidi was right—I was still learning the craft and mistakes were bound to happen here and there.

"Thanks, Heidi," I said softly, reaching over and squeezing

her hand. "I needed that pick-me-up. Leo, not one word to bring back my bad mood."

Hey, I offered you my pipe. I don't do that for just anyone. Besides, it's not me who's a buzz killer. You're thinking of that walking Crayola, Ted. Where did he run off to, anyway? We could always send him to check the crypt without risking ourselves directly.

My wax golem wasn't going anywhere near the cemetery while I sat home safe inside the cottage. It was one thing for Heidi and me to make a quick run in and out, but it was another thing entirely for the six feet, seven-inch gentle giant to walk through the tombstones unprotected. With my luck, someone would spot him rattling someone's bones and think he'd crawled out of a hole considering his relatively stiff stride.

I guess I never thought of Ted along the lines of Night of the Living Dead. *Hey, do you think we can get him cast as an extra on "The Walking Dead"? Think of the money we could make each week, then think of the huge pile of premium organic catnip it could buy. Raven, you finally might be onto something that could keep us in the style to which I could easily become accustomed.*

Leo had definitely inhaled too much concentrated smoke from his catnip pipe. I stood and walked into the kitchen, quickly stacking our dishes into the sink. The exterior of the house left a lot to be desired, but Nan's exquisite taste for interior design was top notch. The kitchen was as modern as one could possibly make it, with granite countertops and the latest brushed stainless-steel appliances. Somehow, she'd successfully integrated antique pieces of furniture through the rest of the one-story cottage, the bedroom loft included.

The living room's coffee table was the central point of the house, with intricate hand carved engravings on every square inch. There were hidden drawers throughout, though a single one in particular protected the family grimoire. Currently, the hex bag was tucked into a smaller drawer for safekeeping. The ward on this table was varied and dramatic. No one but me or one of my most trusted allies could access its secrets.

We'll destroy the bag when we know that Caroline Abigail Whitley didn't turn into some ghoulish grave robber who wants to burn this town to the ground. If I remember correctly, she's spiteful enough to try it, too.

"I know this wasn't how you planned on spending your Friday night," Heidi said, standing from the couch to give herself a once-over. She nodded to herself in approval and to signal that she was ready to go. "I don't mind being second choice, though."

"At least I wasn't the one who had to cancel on Liam this time around." I grabbed the satchel that Ted had brought to me earlier. It contained amaranth, an herb that was meant for protection against evil spirits. It would have been more effective concentrated into a potion if I'd had enough time to make one. I'd requested the material component from Ted right before Liam called to tell me that we needed to postpone our date until tomorrow night. "The mayor requested an emergency meeting with the entire town council, including Liam. He wanted to go over the Fourth of July parade and what needed to be done to make sure the festival went off without a hitch, unlike the last one that featured a murderous clown."

Don't even mention those evil band of jesters. With your batting average, you're liable to conjure one up just by thinking about them, and then we'll be dealing with a ghoul and a hideous clown specter. I can only deal with so much evil at any given time.

"Poor Liam," Heidi said, twisting her cap on backward and making herself look like some kind of West Coast Goth Barbie.

"I heard that the mayor's wife is visiting her sister in Ohio, and that he has no idea what to do with himself without her to boss him around. Liam is sweet to go along with the town council to give the mayor something to do this evening."

Liam Drake *was* a good man. Of that, there was no doubt.

A warmth spread over me at the thought of the man I was currently seeing and slowly assimilating to my life. Liam had no idea that I was a witch, and that was probably a good thing considering that he was the sheriff of Paramour Bay.

Don't get me wrong.

I'd gone back and forth over the decision to tell him the truth, but he had more of a rather no-nonsense attitude toward the natural laws governing life. In his world, magic didn't exit. I'd decided he might have a bit of trouble accepting that the supernatural realm not only existed, but that it existed all around him. I really didn't want to destroy his entire belief system. And then there was the glaring fact that I wasn't ready for our relationship to end.

I feel a hairball coming up. Are we ready to die yet?

Don't mind Leo.

He had trouble accepting that I was dating the sheriff of Paramour Bay in the first place. Technically, Leo would feel that way about any human being. He thought I was putting my life and that of the supernatural realm in jeopardy by exposing my secret life in such an intimate way.

I should get a plaque made that reads "Leo is always right" and hang it on the wall next to the door. That way you'll be reminded of that reality every time you walk out of this cottage. Better yet, I can just point at it during discussions.

"Not happening, Leo," I quipped, feeling better and better about this evening. Liam and the town council would be busy having a business dinner at the mayor's house, which put the odds in our favor that no one would see us sneaking into the cemetery. We'd be in and out in under ten minutes, hopefully with the discovery that Catherine Abigail Whitley's tomb hadn't been disturbed within her family's crypt. It would prove Leo wrong and that this particular ring was just another copy of the original design. "Heidi, put this amaranth underneath your shirt. Rub it on the fabric so that the fragments touch your skin."

I'd taken a pinch of amaranth out of the satchel and sprinkled some of it into the palm of Heidi's hand. Ted had informed me that he'd pulled the entire plant from its soil during a full moon this past summer, following the age-old practice that involved witches warding off evil spirits who lurk in the darkness. I had no idea where Ted was able to obtain some of the material components I needed for my various enchantments, hexes, and wards that I cast when needed, but I'd decided it was better to be kept in the dark rather than be drawn into his world.

Wise choice. Hey, rub some of that amaranth on my fur, would you? What am I? Chopped liver?

"I'm coming, I'm coming," I said, finally making my way over to Leo after I'd confirmed that Heidi had followed my instructions. She was human, and she didn't have the ability to protect herself that way Leo and I did under strenuous supernatural situations. "Here. Let's get you rubbed down, Leo. I'm still hoping that we're taking these extra precautions for naught."

How would you explain Caroline Abigail Whitley's sapphire ring being left in a fifty-cent bin at some garage sale if someone didn't steal it off the woman's cold skeletal phalange or if the woman herself hadn't risen from the dead as a ghoul?

"I wouldn't explain it that way," I replied, having given this some thought. I'm pretty sure I was on to something. "I think it's more likely that her ring was more of a common design than she was willing to admit or that the jeweler made more than one copy and sold them off as one of a kind. Karen somehow ended up with it in her stash of costume jewelry through a perfectly ordinary set of circumstances."

"I'm with Raven," Heidi chimed in, joining us at the door. She'd turned her hat back around and definitely looked like a proper grave robber. Speaking of graves, I had tucked the ring into the front pocket of my black jeans. Neither one of us were taking our purses. This was a quick excursion that shouldn't take long…twenty minutes tops. "I never thought I'd say this, but are we ready to go sneak into the graveyard and go ghoul hunting?"

Does Heidi seem a bit too excited for this type of excursion into the cemetery or is it just me?

Leo and I both watched in dismay as Heidi opened the door with a whistle and not a care in the world that we might be about to confront a monstrously evil supernatural being.

It did concern me a bit that Heidi thought it would be fun to go ghoul hunting, but she worked with numbers all day. That alone would have anyone wanting to deal with floating phantoms, so I'd cut her a break.

"Well, Leo," I replied, setting the satchel on the entry table with resignation before grabbing my keys, "let's go and make sure I didn't flub up another spell."

Sure. That's what we're doing…making sure you didn't incorrectly cast a spell. I give you credit, Raven. You have the ability to make even the direst of situations sound like a ride on a carousel. This is not going to be a snipe hunt. I just want to go on record that if we find out you conjured up a soul-eating ghoul from the depths of the ninth pit of Hades…I'm not beneath throwing Skippy or his friends at it to buy us a little time. Now, as Heidi said—let's go ghoul hunting. Sushi sounds good right about now.

Chapter Three

I SHOULD'VE EATEN a little of the catnip I smoked before this ghoul hunting excursion. I heard the minty sanity-saver actually helps prevent heartburn. Did you know that? Maybe if I had, I wouldn't have a ball of fire stuck in my throat. This acid reflux is hotter than Hades.

"This is really freaking cool," Heidi whispered in complete awe, gradually skimming the white beam spilling from her flashlight over the various-sized tombstones just inside the wrought iron fence surrounding the graveyard. Some were square, some were in the shape of crosses, and there were even a few moss-covered black stones that had cracked and chipped with age. Leo had mentioned that the larger family crypts were located toward the back of this foggy parcel of land that the city had set aside long ago to give the dead their final resting place. "The last time I broke into a graveyard this late at night was back in high school. What was his name? Oh, yeah. Tommy Poplar, and he was so—"

I used the back of my hand to smack Heidi on the arm, the small rebuke receiving an audible *ouch* in reply.

Wow.

I just realized that I was becoming more and more like my mother every day.

Dear Sweet Angel of Mercy—don't talk such blasphemy in a

graveyard.

Leo's love/hate relationship with my mother's renewed interest in Paramour Bay continued to be rather rocky for Leo and me.

That would be the second time tonight that you've sugarcoated the truth, Raven. It didn't work earlier, and it's not going to work now. The readers should know that your mother's demeanor is on par with a soul-eating ghoul. Possibly worse. I need to give that some thought.

Now wasn't the time to get into an argument about my mother or her motives for spending more time in town. We were currently still standing outside the crooked wrought-iron gate of the cemetery, and we'd yet to step on consecrated ground.

Technically, the ground wasn't truly consecrated in every sense of the word.

This cemetery allowed people of all faiths or lack thereof to be buried here. A true consecrated burial ground contained only members of a certain faith. That wasn't quite what the town's forefathers had in mind when they'd established this plot of land for the burial of their families due to the various religions of the local residents.

I'd only ever been to this cemetery once, and that was the day we'd buried Nan. The graveyard looked completely different in the obscure shadows of the night with the patches of fog low to the ground, and it didn't help that the drifting clouds above kept most of the moonlight tucked in tight behind its patchwork blanket.

You know, maybe this soul-eating ghoul doesn't much care for the taste of charred fur. Having severe heartburn might come in handy for once. Caroline Abigail Whitley always struck me as a woman with very particular tastes when it came to her evening meal.

"Tell us more about Mrs. Whitley," I suggested with a cautious scan of the headstones, thinking that maybe having Leo talk while we walked through the cemetery might make this graveyard tour a little less intimidating. Also, it wouldn't hurt to know more about the woman we were going to visit tonight. "If she was the wife of a founder of this town, she obviously came from old family money."

Caroline Abigail Whitley had married into a family of wealth, but she had been born into a very affluent family herself. She married a man by the name of Warren Lawrence Whitley, whose family had been heavily invested in the various marinas and seaports around the area. They were both used to the finer things in life, but it was said that Mrs. Whitley was somewhat difficult to please. Some said she and the husband had a rather distant marriage due to his constant wandering eye. Others say it was an arranged marriage between the families, and that the Missus wanted nothing to do with Mr. Whitley from the start. One thing was for certain…Warren Lawrence Whitley certainly kept his wife in the finest clothes and jewelry to which a woman of her stature was accustomed.

"What's Leo saying?" Heidi whispered, the first one to go through the semi-open rusted gate. "I hate that I can't hear him in situations like these. I'm just saying that he better meow at the top of his lungs if he spots some ghost floating off in the distance. The fun is beginning to wear off, especially since the blonde is usually the first to die off in horror flicks that start out just like this."

I quickly caught Heidi up on the interesting tidbits of the Whitley family history as we fell into step beside one another. She had been gung-ho at the start of this adventure, but being in the immersive eerie setting of a dark foggy graveyard deep in the night had a way of changing one's outlook. It had certainly changed mine.

Where were the crickets?

Where was the light coastal breeze we'd been breathing just outside the wrought-iron fence of the cemetery?

Where was the occasional night owl that liked to ask everyone its favorite question—who?

It was unnervingly silent as we continued to weave our way through the individual tombstones, mindful of stepping on top of someone's grave. The drifting clouds parted every now and then to allow the radiant moonlight to brush over a granite headstone here and there, but the lingering effect was an unsettling collage.

You can let Heidi know that the first indicator to run is when all she sees are my orange and black strands of fur floating in the beam of her flashlight. It's an affliction, suddenly vanishing in response to terror. I can't help it, really. Upon further thought, I'd say it's a rather magnificent instinctive reaction in keeping with the innate desire to live. I can fix my own sushi right here in Paramour Bay.

The slightest scraping sound could be heard directly ahead of us, causing all three of us to stop in our tracks. Heidi quickly swung the flashlight a couple of inches to the right and left, but there didn't seem to be anything out of place. Leo had blipped in and out so fast, he reminded me of an old-time black and white movie that constantly flickered. He *had* left a few floating strands of fur in the white beam of the flashlight as he'd completely disappeared altogether.

As I said, it's an affliction. I don't see anything yet. Do you? It could be Skippy or one of his ninja minions playing games, taking advantage of our situation. I should have rigged a few squirrel traps.

We could offer him up as a sacrificial offering. Do ghouls eat squirrels?

Something scurried across the path in front of us, immediately garnering panic in me and Heidi. We stepped back as fast as we could, Heidi barely keeping hold of her flashlight. I wasn't so fortunate in the grace department, and I ended up flailing my arms in mini-circles when I realized I'd lost my balance. My effort was fruitless, though, and I eventually ended up on my backside in the grass.

Ah, my nemesis! See, Raven? I knew Skippy would take advantage of the situation and attempt to rile my anger. Come back here, you rapscallion!

"For goodness sake, stand up before a hand pops out of the ground and grabs ahold of you," Heidi muttered a bit breathlessly after we'd both somewhat recovered. Sure enough, Leo had taken off after Skippy in more of a headlong wobble than a flat-out run. His weight issue tended to prevent him from being faster than his prey, but it wasn't like he would ever hurt another animal, anyway. He was all talk and no follow-through. "I should have asked you if there were such things as zombies. The fun has been totally zapped out of this ghost tour, and now it's just downright creepy around here."

I took ahold of Heidi's outstretched hand, quickly getting to my feet and brushing off the old grass clippings. Whoever maintained the grounds of the cemetery must have mowed recently.

"I don't think you really want to know the real answer to that zombie question," I replied quietly, pondering over what Heidi's version of a zombie would look like. Nan had used a necromancy spell to keep Leo from crossing over into the afterlife, so it was a safe bet that the same could be done with a human. Talk about upsetting the balance of things. "Let's just keep walking back toward the crypts. They shouldn't be too far away, and Leo knows where we'll be. He'll catch up once Skippy gives him a run for his money."

We both started forward ever so slowly, but we finally picked up speed and began crossing the cemetery at a brisk pace. Neither one of us wanted to be in the graveyard any longer than necessary.

"Look," Heidi finally whispered, not even needing the use of her flashlight anymore. The clouds had parted by the time we reached the back of the huge parcel the cemetery sat on. Sure enough, numerous family crypts were lined up near a chest-high cobblestone wall with wrought iron spikes not as straight as they should have been sticking out of the top of the surrounding structure. I'm sure in the olden days it prevented grave robbers from looting the tombs of those more affluent in society. "I didn't know that Paramour Bay had so many families who owned these types of burial tombs."

I took the flashlight out of Heidi's hand and focused the white beam onto the plaque of the crypt in front of us to make the names easier to read. Go figure. This particular inscription read *Barnes*.

I knew the family quite well.

We weren't on the best of terms, but that was because Cora Barnes detested my mother with a passion. Cora was married to Desmond Barnes, and they both owned the malt shop next door to my tea shop. They were definitely well off in the bank account area, if you know what I mean. Desmond's family owned a lot of the buildings along River Bay, as well as quite a bit of real estate in the surrounding area.

"It makes sense," I whispered in response before beginning

our cautious stroll parallel to the crypts. The blackness of the cement seemed almost like a damp coat of paint. "Barnes, Sanders, and the Bends all probably have crypts with their ancestors buried here. I don't recall any Whitleys living in the immediate area, but I'm still meeting a few of the town's residents every other day. I'll ask Leo if any descendants remain in town, if he ever tires of chasing wind."

Paramour Bay's population was currently at three hundred and fifty-six now that Heidi had moved here last month. There could be a Whitley or two still in the more prominent neighborhoods that consisted mostly of the waterfront properties. Those residents weren't known to do their own tea shopping, if you get my drift.

It was something we could check out tomorrow, if need be. The ring in my pocket could still simply be a replica made by a long distant relative of Mrs. Whitley or there might have been copies made and sold as originals by an unscrupulous jeweler.

There was a really good chance that Leo had been overreacting to the accidental discovery of the ring.

Right?

"There," Heidi said quietly, pointing her finger toward a crypt that was practically in the middle of the back row. It was somewhat larger than the others, but it was what one would expect of the Whitleys whom Leo had described. After all, they were basically the founders of the small town and had garnered the respect of the newly arrived residents who'd followed to plant their own family roots. "You're the witch. You should do the honors on opening the doors. That is, if they don't fall apart. Look at the state of that wood."

What Heidi was trying to say was that I was the one who had the ability to fend off a physical attack with the energy I harnessed in the palm of my right hand. Unfortunately, I wasn't quite sure a strong surge of power from the earth would do a thing to something as ethereal as a ghost. That was the main reason why we'd rubbed amaranth underneath our shirts, and I could only hope that the material component did its reputed job.

My palm was a bit sweaty, but the reason had nothing to do with an innate sense of danger and more to do with the level of humidity. It was still eerily quiet, but that would help in detecting the slightest of noises that could potentially signal we weren't alone in this graveyard. I wiped my hands down my thighs before reaching forward and gently lifting the latch that held the two old and weathered wooden doors together covering the entrance to the crypt.

Raven!

I screamed.

I'll admit that it wasn't my best moment, but Leo's voice had sliced through the deafening silence with a lethal swipe. I will hand it to Heidi, though. She didn't leave me hanging. In the belief that I'd actually encountered the ghost of Caroline Abigail Whitley, my best friend had wrapped a death grip around my arm and yanked me back from the partially opened entry to the crypt.

Where is she? Is she coming after us? Run for your lives!

Leo disappeared in the blink of an eye while Heidi was still trying to pull me away from the crypt. My adrenaline was pumping, and my heart was beating hard against my chest, but there had been no soul-eating ghoul inside the tomb.

"Heidi, it's okay. We're safe," I said in reassurance, purposefully shining the flashlight on the cracked opening between the two doors. "See? There's nothing there. Leo just scared me when he suddenly called out my name like some lunatic."

Heidi's blue eyes were so wide that they appeared to be glowing, and she rested a palm over her heart before finally releasing her tight grip on my arm. She then held up her other hand as she leaned over to catch her breath.

"Leo," I called out in a harsh whisper, looking all around us. "Come back here this minute!"

Over here.

There was still enough moonlight that I could see Leo's head pop out from behind a headstone around forty feet away from the crypt.

Did she try to eat your soul? Wait. Are you even you or are you some soulless Raven who's doomed to roam the earth alone for all eternity?

"Stop that crazy talk. Right now," I admonished, annoyed that my own familiar had almost given me a heart attack at the young age of thirty.

You're definitely you. I'd recognized that tone anywhere. Why did you scream like your soul was being consumed by a banshee?

Leo sauntered over to us, rubbing against Heidi's leg until she ran a hand down his back in comfort.

"I was lifting the latch off the doors to the crypt in stone cold silence when you materialized out of thin air and screamed my name." I was finally able to somewhat relax now that nothing had come floating out from the Whitley family crypt. It helped that Leo was now in attendance and couldn't spontaneously appear from nowhere. "Let me just make sure that Mrs. Whitley's personal resting—"

I didn't spontaneously appear out of nowhere, dear Raven. I ran into this talking raccoon, and he was trying to warn me about…well, I might have freaked out a bit when the garbage eater sounded like he'd been a pet of a New York mafia don. Honestly, I don't know what he was trying to warn me about. What respectable raccoon talks like he's a Jersey gangster? I did the only thing I could…I ran for my life.

"How much catnip did you go through before we left the house?" I asked in disbelief, wondering if I shouldn't make an emergency appointment for Leo to see Dr. Jameson. Leo might have had his battles with the local wildlife, but he'd never heard them talk as if they had human voices. The local vet had already dealt with my frantic calls about the possibility of overdosing on catnip. He'd repeatedly told me that no such thing could happen, but it was a fair bet that he'd never encountered a cat who special ordered the most powerful species of the minty herb from Honduras. "Please tell me there are still a few leftovers from today's shipment."

You make it sound as if I have some sort of problem, which I adamantly deny. You don't hear me telling you to stop drinking coffee after the fifth pot, now do you?

Just so we're clear, I do *not* drink five pots of coffee a day. Two, maybe. Fine, maybe three, but that's with the help of Beetle at the store and some of the sample urns I make for the visitors at the shop. Leo was just trying to take the spotlight off him and the fact that he had hallucinated talking raccoons.

"I can breathe again," Heidi announced as though it was a revelation to us all. Her affirmation on her health didn't stop her from cautiously glancing over her shoulder to make sure that a zombie hadn't climbed out of a random grave. Her blue gaze finally focused on the partially opened doors to the crypt, and she made a circular motion with her hand. "Let's get this over with. And just so you know, I'm sleeping on your couch tonight."

I can't believe you think I hallucinated a talking raccoon. I mean, that's really low on the list of things I'd want to hallucinate about if given the chance. And why would I give him a New York mafia accent? Raven, Raven, Raven. I don't believe you think these theories through before they come spilling out of your mouth.

"What are you two carrying on about now?" Heidi asked, giving me a soft nudge toward the crypt. "You two are worse than an old married couple."

I resent that comparison. I'm still a vibrant tomcat.

"Leo had a conversation with a talking raccoon," I murmured, carefully aiming the flashlight through the ancient doors of the crypt.

You're making me sound just a bit unbalanced, Raven. Not nice. Not nice, at all.

"How much catnip did you eat, you handsome tomcat?"

Where is that soul-eating ghoul when I need her?

"Don't stroke his ego, Heidi."

We all became quiet really quick when the white beam immediately landed on a bare cement wall. Nudging the doors open a little more, nothing seemed to change in our lines of vision. Finally, each door was practically resting against either wall.

There was nothing here.

Where were the smaller vaults in the walls?

Where were the stone coffins that I'd seen in pictures of above ground crypts just like this one?

Aim the flashlight a smidge bit lower, Raven. A little more. And…there. See? It is a crypt. I'm not so unbalanced after all, am I?

"What. Is. That?" Heidi's adrenaline rush for the unknown must have petered out, because I'm pretty sure she was ready to turn on the heels of those black running shoes and see how much traction she could get from the treads. "I've officially changed my mind. We should have sent Ted."

I'd landed the beam of the flashlight onto a rather large opening with cement stairs that descended into nothing but darkness below. Somewhere down there was the final resting place of Caroline Abigail Whitley. We were no more than twenty feet away from the answers we were seeking, but neither Heidi, Leo, or I could make ourselves take that first step into the inky blackness.

Once more, my hesitancy to walk down inside a crypt where a soul-eating ghoul could be waiting for us proves I'm not unbalanced at all...I just wanted that to go on the record.

There was no telling how long we would have stood in the entrance of the crypt deciding if we were brave enough to descend into the darkness had a deep voice not broken the silence behind us. Needless to say, Leo was the first to dive headlong down the steep staircase into an abyss that most likely contained a soul-eating ghoul.

Chapter Four

I'M HONESTLY NOT sure how we didn't break our necks scurrying down the cement staircase. One minute, we had been above ground. The next…well, we were submersed in the darkness deep within a crypt with the remains of the dead surrounding us.

"It's just me," Rye Dolgiram said quietly in reassurance as he followed us down inside the burial chamber. His deep voice echoed off the chamber walls and sent shivers down my spine with the realization of where we were. Images of the heavy wooden doors closing above and shutting us inside flashed through my mind, but thankfully I could still see a sliver of moonlight illuminating Rye's silhouette on the staircase. "Do I want to know what the three of you doing in the local cemetery at this time of night on a Friday evening?"

Zap him, Raven. Summon up the earth's energy and eviscerate him into a nice pile of ash. Who walks up behind someone in a graveyard without fair warning? What did he expect our reaction to be? Better yet, who walks up behind someone while they're standing just inside the one crypt in a graveyard where a ravenous soul-eating ghoul might be lying in wait? No one but a sadistic nut job who wants to be zapped, that's who. Zap him, Raven!

"Rye, what on earth are you doing here?" I all but demanded, shining the white beam of the flashlight directly into his line of vision. The palm of my hand hadn't warmed in warning of his presence, so that alone told me he wasn't here with bad intent. With that said, I couldn't imagine him randomly taking a stroll by himself in a graveyard on a Friday night at the exact moment as us without there being some extraordinary reason. Something smelled fishy, and it wasn't Leo's breath for once. "You should know better than to sneak up on us in a spooky graveyard. It could very well have ended up poorly for you. Not to mention that we could have fallen down the stairs and broken our necks."

"Yes," Heidi said in reinforcement, her body practically hugging mine since we still didn't know what was inside the burial chamber. She also had a grip on my forearm that might actually leave her handprint in marked bruises. "What she said. Not cool, Rye. Not cool at all. Huge party foul."

The story of Rye Dolgiram was rather long, but I'll cut to the chase and make this quick. He was a warlock of considerable power, and as chance would have it…the adopted son of my Aunt Rowena.

Technically, she was my great-aunt and the only sister to my Nan.

Trust me when I say that Aunt Rowena was one of a kind, but we weren't currently on what one might call good speaking terms. She was theoretically still with a faction of the coven up in Windsor, if you discounted the fact that she was leading that same faction of witches and warlocks against the leadership council of said coven. My immediate family hadn't been in good standing with the coven ever since my Nan's expulsion many years prior to the current difficulties.

A witch war was brewing, and our small branch of the family wanted no part of it.

Bottom line was that I'd come to find out recently that Rye

had been adopted by Aunt Rowena in his teens, and that he'd moved to Paramour Bay many years ago when the council had decided an attempt to discover the identity of his birth parents was paramount. Needless to say, there was only one way to do so—and that was by contacting those involved in the afterlife.

Séances weren't something to be messed with seeing as they opened a two-way portal to the other side, but I highly doubted that was the sole reason for Aunt Rowena's hesitation on that particular subject matter. There was something more to Rye Dolgiram, and we were purposefully being kept in the dark, along with the rest of the coven.

In case you hadn't noticed, Raven, we are sitting here defenseless in the dark. Would you mind postponing this discussion for when we're not about to have our souls sucked out of us by the raging poltergeist of Caroline Abigail Whitley? I can just picture her licking her fingers in delight at how delicious I might be...do you think I would taste like mint?

"You shouldn't be here," I whispered to Rye while complying with Leo's wishes to move this discussion along. I wasn't worried about Leo being a snack for a soul-eating ghoul when he could easily blip out of here with a twitch of his whiskers. Then again, I was really hoping that this place was blocking my ability to harness energy, because the palm of my right hand was still quite cool. Why did it feel as if someone or something was watching our every move? Was there something else here besides us and the dusty skeletal remains of the Whitley family? I began to slowly walk in a circle while aiming the somewhat trembling flashlight over the floor to ceiling square vaults cut into the walls. Heidi was doing her best to shuffle her feet in order to turn with me in sync, afraid we might actually come face to face with a ghoul with a huge gaping maw. "We're...conducting a history lesson on the town founders. We're fine, and you can head back home."

That's the best you could come up with? A history lesson on the town founders? Raven, let Heidi take over on the cover story front. You're liable to end up having us arrested for grave robbing. Considering the sapphire ring of one dead Caroline Abigail Whitley is currently in the front pocket of your jeans, the good ol' sheriff has all the evidence he'd need to throw us all in jail.

"A history lesson?" Rye asked skeptically, confirming Leo's belief that I was really bad at lying. I was, but that was beside the point. "What is down here that is so important it couldn't wait until broad daylight?"

Don't answer him, Raven. I can see it now—he'll steal the priceless gem, lock us in here until the soul-eating ghoul gets her fill, and no one will ever be the wiser to the true story behind our demise. Where's Skippy when I need him? Oh, wait. Do you think the talking raccoon has co-opted his allegiance?

"What priceless gem is Leo talking about?" Rye asked, having heard every word that Leo had been saying since his arrival. After all, he was a warlock. "And did he actually mention a soul-eating ghoul? Oh, I get it. You let him dig into the catnip bag unsupervised again, didn't you?"

Why you...

Heidi was to my right, but Leo had taken up residence on my left side. I could literally feel the wiggle of his backside, which told me he was getting ready to pounce onto Rye.

"Both of you just stop it," I ordered quietly, trying to swallow when the beam of my flashlight landed on two stone coffins sitting on two raised pedestals. Our backs were now to Rye, but I didn't mind. If there any real danger, it was definitely directly in front of us. "Um, Rye. There's something we should tell you."

I vote for zapping him unconscious and leaving his lifeless body here for—

"Come here, handsome," Heidi murmured, leaning down behind me and somehow managing to scoop Leo up into her arms without even a grunt. She must have been keeping up with her yoga. It didn't take her long to settle back into position by my side. "I don't know what you're saying, but let Raven handle this so that we can all get home in one piece. I've had my fill of fun this Friday night. A glass…well, a bottle of wine sounds excellent right about now."

"Seriously, Raven," Rye said, coming to stand by us as he also shone his flashlight on the two main burial coffins of the patriarch and matriarch of the Whitley family. There was no manifestation of ghouls in the corners. That was a good sign, right? "What's going on?"

I might as well bring Rye up to date seeing as we weren't currently ready to have our souls devoured by Caroline Abigail Whitley. He hadn't bought a word of what I'd said, anyway, and I'm pretty sure all Heidi wanted to do was get back safely to the cottage after the scares we'd had tonight.

Not to put a wrench in our plans, but we still need to deal with the talking raccoon.

Rye tilted his head in disbelief as Leo mentioned his hallucination, but I didn't want to waste any more time than we already had in this underground crypt. It was one thing when I thought it was above ground and we could run for our lives if needed, but it was an entirely different situation when we could be locked down here to have our souls consumed by the undead.

"Long story short—I was at the garage sale today, visiting Karen Finley's table. She had this little discount basket of jewelry," I explained quickly, shifting the flashlight to my left hand as I fished out the sapphire ring from my right pocket. I held it up in the light so that Rye could get a better look at the item in question. "Leo is almost one hundred percent sure it's the same ring that was buried with its original owner—Caroline Abigail Whitley."

You're forgetting the part about you giving Heidi a hex bag as a gift for moving into her new office.

"A hex bag?" Rye questioned, real concern lacing his tone as he focused his flashlight on the two stone burial chambers. I really, really tried to not take offense that everyone assumed I couldn't successfully cast a simple spell. "Let me guess. You were attempting to create a warding spell against evil, and you think it might not have gone quite as you originally planned."

At least the resident warlock is quick on the uptake.

Heidi hugged Leo a little closer as she juggled his weight in an attempt to grab the flashlight from my hand. I wasn't sure what she saw that had garnered such a reflex, but it wasn't long before she quickly inhaled in fright. Her echo bounced around the chamber and also had Leo scrambling for a better hold of her shirt.

Sure enough, I saw the same exact horrifying detail she had—the stone lid on top of Caroline Abigail Whitley's resting place was slightly askew.

Had her spirit escaped into the burial chamber?

Had we been duped?

Were our souls about to be sucked out of our bodies?

I hope that was a rhetorical question, because we need to go home right this second. Chop-chop! We'll pack our bags, book a flight to Honduras, and then grab Beetle on the way out of town. He saved for retirement, so he'll have the appropriate funds we need to keep me in the lifestyle I've become accustomed to over these last few decades.

"Let's not overreact," Rye stated firmly, although we all noticed the way he made sure to illuminate every corner of the burial chamber before taking a stride forward for a better look inside the coffin. "What the…"

Heidi and I quickly stepped back in unison when Rye began to try and shove the lid back a bit more, though why he would want to do such a thing was beyond my wildest imagination.

"What are you doing? Stop that!" I whispered fiercely, unable to prevent my voice from resonating throughout the hollow space that most likely harbored a soul-eating ghoul. "Are you crazy? Just see if the ring is still on her finger and then we can make a run for it. I'll destroy the hex bag the minute we get home and—"

"I don't think it's going to be that simple," Rye muttered, after having managed to move the heavy stone lid another couple of inches. He even blinked a few times, as if he wasn't sure what was inside. How could he not recognize a skeleton? "We might just have a major problem on our hands."

Has the resident warlock not been paying attention this entire time? We've had *a problem, and it's most likely in the form of a misty gnarly-looking apparition that will suck out our souls with one gulp. I can't look, and Heidi smells great. Tell her that I love her bodywash, please. I want those to be the last words she hears before we're consumed.*

I forced my legs to move, achieving the few steps forward that I needed to in order to carefully peer inside the stone coffin. I purposefully squinted, as though that would shield me from the horrific view of the skeletal remains that were resting inside. Little by little, I had no choice but to widen my eyes, because I couldn't seem to focus on the expected bones.

"See what I mean?" Rye said, having no choice but to relinquish his flashlight when I snatched it right out of his hands.

"For crying out loud," Heidi chastised with impatience, which usually got the best of her. She came closer, attempting to put Leo on the lid. He was having none of that mess, and I had no doubt that there would be holes in my long-sleeved black t-shirt. "You guys are skeeving me out. Is the ring in there or not? How hard can it be to—"

Sure enough, Heidi was brought up short.

Are we being pranked? That's it, isn't it? Your mother came to town thinking she'd have a bit of fun and set up the talking raccoon gig, brought Rye in on the joke, and then desecrated a coffin. It is a bit overboard, but I'll admit that it was well played. Regina Lattice Marigold, you show yourself right this minute!

We were all as still as the two stone coffins, secretly hoping that Leo was right and that this was all some sort of distasteful hoax. Unfortunately, not even my mother would take things this far to prove a point. That didn't stop us from giving her time to show herself, but we all finally had to admit that we were in real, real trouble.

You see, Caroline Abigail Whitley's ring was not in the coffin…but neither were her remains.

"Now might be a good time for me confess," Rye said reluctantly while he shifted with unease. He reclaimed his flashlight. "You see, I—"

I knew it! Where is she? Regina Lattice Marigold, show yourself, you miscreant!

"Regina isn't here, Leo," Rye replied, tilting his head back as if he were reluctant to acknowledge whatever it was he was trying to confess. "This one is all on me."

Confess?

That's what he said. Let him do it, Raven. Confess your sins, you evil doer!

Had he been the one to desecrate a founding member's burial chambers?

I couldn't bring myself to believe something so horrendous, so I braced myself for whatever I was about to hear. I was still in somewhat shock that we were dealing with an empty coffin, so it was rather easy to allow Leo to take the lead.

This is Rowena's doing, isn't it? She's trying to build a ghoul army to take down the other faction of the coven, and she's having you dig up the remains of the dead to—

"I might have allowed Leo to consume a bit too much catnip before we started out here tonight," I grudgingly affirmed, shooting Leo a look that told him his flair for the dramatic wasn't helping the situation. "Rye, what did you do?"

"I made an attempt to contact one of my ancestors last night."

I did not see that one coming.

"I set up a séance and tried to open up a channel of communication between the living and the dead. I don't think it was your hex bag that was responsible for the missing remains of Caroline Abigail Whitley. I'm pretty sure that consequence lies solely at my feet, but I want you to know that I'll do whatever it takes to rectify this situation. Go on home. Pretend you didn't see a thing, and I'll make sure that things are set right before the next sunrise."

Did you hear that, Raven? Did you?

Leo seemed somewhat on the verge of an anxiety attack and had begun pacing back and forth on top of the stone lid, which only seemed to unnerve him further. Heidi might have muttered *oh dear*, but I couldn't hear her muted whisper over the pounding of blood in my ears. Also, I was doing my very best to make sure I didn't hyperventilate.

I'm pretty sure I heard the resident warlock say he opened up the door between the living and the dead, Raven. I'm going to be sick. Here it comes…the biggest hairball I've ever regurgitated. Is it a bad thing if I hack it up into the coffin? I mean, who would actually say to themselves—other than one of your relatives—that it would be a good idea to open communication between the living and the dead? This bumbling warlock did, that's who—all by himself. In a town of three hundred and fifty-six people…three hundred and fifty-four of them being regular everyday humans. Wasn't that so smart of him?

"Leo, I made sure to take precautions," Rye said in defense of himself. Had he taken the proper precautions? I'd also finished casting a protection ward against evil, so I'd say it was a fifty-fifty chance as to which one of us was responsible for…well, I wasn't exactly sure what we were dealing with here. Was it possible that our spells interfered with one another? With that said, opening up a door for any and all spirits to walk through hadn't been the best of ideas. "If something or someone did slip through, I can contain it."

I'll tell you what we're dealing with, you two bumbling spell-flubbers—a zombie apocalypse. But you two couldn't just stick with regular zombies, could you? You had to go include talking raccoons, and now those garbage scroungers plan to take over the world! Hack…hack…and here comes the hairball. I'm going to be cursed for desecrating a coffin.

Chapter Five

"**P**LEASE TELL ME that I have a hangover from drinking too much wine last night and that my raging headache is the sole reason I had a horrible nightmare about an empty crypt, a missing ring, and—"

Go ahead and say it.

Leo sat immobile in his favorite lounging spot by the front window. He was still sulking because I didn't believe him about last night's talking raccoon encounter, though his intense gaze was glued to the front yard as if we were about to be invaded by a horde of zombies.

Talking raccoons. Yes, a raccoon tried to start a conversation with me. It happened. Now, please tell my beloved Heidi that I'll watch for the herd of zombie garbage scrappers and give her fair warning so that she can make a run for it. Skippy will finally be able to witness my heroic death.

"Leo, stop being so dramatic," I chided him with a yawn, pouring coffee into two mugs for both me and Heidi. We were going to need some sort of fuel to come up with a plan to rectify the small problem we'd encountered in the graveyard last night. I had a revelation as I combed back over the spell I'd cast into Heidi's hex bag, and I'm nearly certain that I'd done everything to perfection. "Heidi, you aren't hungover. Come to think of it, you didn't even have a sip of wine after we got home from the cemetery. But I do have good news, because I got to thinking that maybe we're not dealing with simple witchcraft, after all."

Thinking before your first sip of coffee is never wise, my dear Raven. Haven't we learned anything in these past few months?

Heidi was currently sitting on one of the stools at the kitchen island slumped over the counter with her forehead pressed against her forearms. It was my overly optimistic statement that had her lifting her head, but at least she gave Leo a quick glance over her shoulder.

"Leo, give her a chance to tell us what she came up with, because I'm not quite ready for a zombie apocalypse this morning." Heidi leaned forward in desperation even more, wiggling her fingers at me to signal that she was in dire need of some caffeine. "What do you mean that you don't think it was *simple* witchcraft? I hate to break this to you, but skeletal remains just don't open the lid to their own burial chamber and walk off through the graveyard rattling their bones as they take a stroll."

That was the exact point I was trying to make.

I joined Heidi at the island after sliding a mug into her grab-by little hands. It was best I start from the beginning, but I was going to have to make this quick. I'd already given Liam a call to meet us at the cemetery around lunchtime.

You did what? No, don't answer that question. I'll just hear random facts that aren't related in the least, leaving me no choice but to blame that necromancy spell your grandmother used to prevent me from crossing into the afterlife. It's more of a catchall catastrophe, really. More damage was done than we'd thought…I'm actually brain dead, aren't I?

"Leo, just hear me out for a minute," I requested, holding up a hand while I took a fortifying sip of my coffee. I had to close my eyes as the delicious rich beverage warmed my tattered soul.

There was a reason for that, too. "Listen, you two. I don't believe Caroline Abigail Whitley was turned into a ghoul, a zombie, or anything else like that. I think her skeletal remains were stolen from the Whitley family crypt, along with all the valuable jewelry she was laid to rest with so many years ago."

Heidi had used my slippers that she'd confiscated to shift the stool so that she was facing me, but she didn't say a word at my announcement. As a matter of fact, she blinked those baby blue eyes of hers quite a few times while attempting to digest my new theory along with its implications. She even took another sip of her coffee as if she was ready to hear more. It wasn't long after I failed to continue that she shared an odd look with Leo that told me neither one of them was buying what I was selling.

You've got nothing more to say?

"Think about it," I said, setting my mug on the granite counter so that I could get my point across. "I created the hex bag two nights ago, the same evening that Rye attempted to do a séance. Twenty-four hours later, we walked into a crypt to find that Caroline Abigail Whitley's remains were no longer in her final resting place. If either one of us were responsible for the rising of the dead, something dire would have occurred within that same twenty-four hours. Black magic has consequences for the caster. Nothing has happened."

If you hadn't moved for centuries, don't you think it might take you longer than a day to get your joints working again? Have you considered that the consequences are pending?

"Whatever he said," Heidi murmured in agreement from behind her coffee cup.

It's wishful thinking, which is the one activity you shouldn't be doing without having finished your first cup of coffee. We've talked about this on numerous occasions, Raven.

"I'm serious." How could Leo and Heidi not connect the dots? "I just spoke with Liam not even fifteen minutes ago. Don't you think if there was an animated undead creature of some sort roaming around Paramour Bay that he wouldn't have been the first one to catch an earful about it? Nothing happens in this town without Liam hearing something first."

Considering there's at least one novice witch, a practicing warlock, a rather brilliant familiar, and a giant walking Crayola roaming around the streets of this coastal town without the good ol' sheriff connecting the dots, I would have to disagree with that not-so-obvious assessment. And that's not even mentioning the witch's coven he stumbled into, the insane war brewing between the factions of said coven, and the fact that there's an entire supernatural realm that exists right under the good ol' sheriff's nose. It's quite astonishing, really. He doesn't have the slightest idea what goes on in his town.

"That's not fair, Leo, and you know it."

"Raven has a point," Heidi said, finally backing me up. "I mean, no one has gone missing. Liam would have immediately warned Raven. On top of that, what type of respectable poltergeist leaves a genuine sapphire ring in a half-dollar basket at a garage sale?"

I see Heidi's point, but the same could be said for a human. Who in their right mind would leave jewelry worth tens of thousands of dollars in a cheap basket with a sign that read fifty cents apiece? No one, that's who.

"Leo, are there any descendants of the Whitley family who are still alive and reside in or around Paramour Bay?" I reached for my coffee now that we were finally getting somewhere. "I understand that anyone could have gone inside the crypt and stole…well, everything inside, but doesn't it stand to reason that it would be a Whitley wanting to gain access to the family jewels? Who else would know the jewels were buried with them?"

Everyone, that's who. It's not like it was kept a secret. As for the Whitleys, there are a few remaining households near the waterfront properties, but those descendants favor the city over a small coastal town that doesn't offer them the entertainment and access. I hate to pop your balloon, but they're worth several thousand times more than that one sapphire ring. They would have no reason to rob the grave of their great-great-great-great grandmother, let alone steal her skeletal remains and a few trinkets.

"I might love me some diamonds, rubies, and sapphires, but I have to say that desecrating the grave of an old ancestor is pretty morbid," Heidi interjected with a roll of her eyes before taking her mug over to the couch in the living room. She settled into the oversized cushions with a sigh, very content to be in the safety of the cottage. "Personally, I like the idea that we're dealing with human greed over some soul-eating ghoul. So, what's the plan?"

You two seem to be conveniently forgetting about the talking raccoon. We have a real problem on our hands, and you two seem to have your heads in the garbage can right along with them.

That talking raccoon was the only snag in my theory. I'd have to do a little research about that stash of premium organic catnip Leo had shipped here from Honduras. Maybe there was some online forum where pet owners went to talk about side effects from such an exotic intoxicating herb.

Really? You've sunk so low that you don't believe your most trusted advisor? That is—

I'd joined Heidi in the living room to finish our conversation, plus to enjoy the rest of my coffee before getting ready for the day. I hadn't even made it to my favorite oversized red velvet pillow in front of the fireplace when Leo had all but fallen out of his cat bed backing up from something he'd seen outside.

Look, Raven!

Leo had managed to bark his order out right before he lost his footing and all but fell to the floor with an unceremonious thud. He certainly wasn't quick on his feet, but I don't think I've ever seen him vanish from one spot and reappear in another so fast. By the time my focus had landed on him back on top of his cat bed, he had his nose pressed tightly against the window.

The talking raccoon is gone! Vanished. Vamoosed. Raven, you have to be quicker than that if you wish to uncover the supernatural.

"Are you saying you saw the talking raccoon again?" I made my way over to the window overlooking the front lawn, quickly scanning the black wrought iron fence that surrounded the property. The only thing I spotted was rather hard to miss, and that was Ted as he walked by the window without even a sideways glance. "We'll ask Ted if he saw anything when he came around the side of the house."

Ted is probably the reason the garbage eater scampered away.

Leo plopped back onto his cat bed with a disappointing sigh.

I did not imagine that talking raccoon, Raven. And only flubbed-up spells can lead to talking garbage disposals.

"I'm not saying you completely imagined the raccoon, but you've also never tried that Honduras premium organic catnip before," I pointed out, not wanting to rule anything out. "If Rye and I had nothing to do with the empty crypt, then we'd have to come up with a reasonable explanation as to why you had a literal conversation with a raccoon."

"Is it possible that the raccoon is a familiar?" Heidi asked right when Ted knocked on the door. He never used the doorbell. I wasn't sure what his aversion was to the white button. "Or maybe Nan cursed a door-to-door salesman who used to be an annoying human. That could have happened, right?"

And you thought I had a flair for the dramatic.

"Good morning," Ted announced after I'd swung open the door.

I'd mentioned this before, but Ted had come with the house. He lived in the small dwelling on the back of the property near the water's edge, and he was very succinct in the way he spoke.

Dwelling? It's a shed, Raven. Most people put lawnmowers in them, not their henchmen.

"Oh, you're just cranky because no one else has seen the talking raccoon with our own eyes. And to answer your question, Heidi, I haven't yet found a spell in the family grimoire that can turn a human into an animal of any sort."

"Do I want to know why you were looking for one?" Heidi asked with a laugh, sitting up a little straighter and saying hello to Ted. "Ted, my man. How's it hanging?"

"It's going fine, Ms. Heidi."

You should let Heidi know that we don't have some sort of bat signal that lets us know when another of our kind is around, and no one in their right mind would choose a rabid garbage disposal as a familiar.

Ted had a basket in his extremely large hand, which I knew contained material components for spells I usually liked to dabble in on Saturdays. Now that I had part-time help at the tea shop, I could stay at home and work on creating the holistic blends needed for those local residents in need of some herbal remedies…with an added touch of magic, of course.

"Did you, by chance, see a raccoon in the front yard?" I asked, sliding back a bit on the hardwood floor with my fuzzy socks. It certainly wasn't the time of year to be wearing them, but they were so cozy that I couldn't bring myself to store them away for the summer quite yet.

"Raccoons are nocturnal, Ms. Raven."

For being made of congealed wax, Ted certainly is a walking encyclopedia of useless facts. You tell that oversized grey crayon that—

"Yes, raccoons are nocturnal," I replied with a smile, closing the door now that Ted had ducked underneath the doorway and made his way inside. "Leo had a…well, a run-in with a rather verbose raccoon last night. He thought he saw the same one outside a few moments ago."

I thought I saw? Your choice of words leaves a lot to be desired.

"I did not see a raccoon." Ted slowly made his way over to the coffee table, setting the white wicker basket down on the polished surface in the precise manner and placement that had almost become obsessive. He literally shifted the basket three times in quick succession until the side was in perfect alignment with one of the hand carved grooves. "I will be heading into town now."

Ted had what one might call an odd crush on a mannequin in the boutique a couple of storefronts down from the teashop. None of the townsfolk really talked about it much, very kindly accepting that Ted was a bit different from the norm. His kind heart for all things was hard to miss, and he always had a crooked smile for everyone who said hello.

"Should I see a raccoon, I will ask if it knows Leo."

Sweet angel of mercy, I'm surrounded by—

"Ted, do you know the Whitley family?" Heidi asked, having no idea she'd just saved Ted from a mouthful of meows. She shifted to her side and propped herself up with her right elbow.

"They were one of the founding families of the town."

"Yes, I do."

I hope Heidi has a pair of pliers. Otherwise, we'll be here all day trying to extract information from this oversized candle. Ted has only been in existence for ten years. Trust me, he doesn't know anything that can—

"Mr. Arthur Whitley is an odd character."

Who? And did Ted just call someone odd? That is by far the strongest case I've ever seen of the pot calling the kettle black.

"What exactly do you mean by odd?" I asked, when what I really wanted to know was how he knew an Arthur Whitley. As far as I was aware, none of the Whitley family ever came into town. "And how old is this Arthur?"

I walked around the couch and took a seat at the opposite end of Heidi. Between Leo and Ted, they really were a wealth of information. Once I had a conversation with Liam early this afternoon, I would be armed with all the knowledge I'd need in order to figure out which spell to cast to find the answers to the mystery of the empty crypt.

Why don't we make sure your initial spell isn't the cause of the current apocalypse before you go casting another, shall we, butterfingers?

"Mr. Arthur must be in his late seventies."

Ted tugged on his jacket when he was done fidgeting with the black cloth he'd laid over the roots and herbs inside the basket. The fabric had to be just so before he was satisfied with the presentation. I couldn't let him leave just yet, though.

"Why is Mr. Arthur odd, Ted?"

Wake me when this single syllable interrogation is over. I figure it'll be dinnertime by then.

"Mr. Arthur is what some might call paranoid."

If you say that the old geezer reminds you of me, I won't be responsible for my actions.

I couldn't help but laugh, and I shifted on the couch until it was easy for me to see Leo on the windowsill. All Ted and Heidi could hear were several raspy meows that Leo had emitted, so I repeated his sentiment before I reassured him that wasn't the case.

"Leo, I don't think you're paranoid. Things did get a bit intense last night, though. Think about it—a spooky graveyard, patches of fog, little moonlight, and an empty crypt. You ran after Skippy in the middle of it all, and your emotions were running high. You could have imagined it."

Leo tilted his head until the longest and most crooked whisker was pointed toward the ceiling. The tip of his tail that resembled a hanger tried its best to stand straight up, failing miserably.

Skippy! That's it! He somehow blackmailed a raccoon into his scheme of debauchery. It's very easy nowadays to dupe humans. He could have stolen a phone with his little grubby hands and made it seem as if the raccoon could talk. It makes perfect sense. That scoundrel is going to pay for this!

Leo disappeared in a puff of floating hairs before I could tell him that the odds of Skippy being able to pull something like that off was very unrealistic. Then again, a lot of things about my life were pretty unrealistic.

"Ted, we didn't find Caroline Abigail Whitley's remains inside the family crypt," I said, turning my focus back to the conversation at hand.

"Perhaps you looked in the wrong crypt, Ms. Raven."

Heidi hid her smiled behind her coffee cup.

"No, Ted. We definitely looked in the right crypt and the

right coffin. Caroline Abigail Whitley's remains are undeniably missing."

Ted tilted his square chin as his dark eyes regarded me with curiosity.

"I will ask Ivan about this new mystery of yours."

Both Heidi and I sat in silence at first, but Ted didn't bother to elaborate.

"Ivan?"

"Who is Ivan?"

Both Heidi and I had exchanged confused looks and spoke at the same time. Ted had a tendency of dropping bombshells, and this moment was no exception. For living on the property, Ted certainly kept his personal life well under wraps. Granted, I'd learned it was best not to ask too many questions. Yes, everyone in town was aware he was in love with a mannequin, but the reason for late-night dinners and not coming home until the wee hours was something I'd postponed learning about.

"Ivan takes care of the cemetery grounds."

Ivan? I'd never heard the name before, though I'd mentioned before there were still a few of the town's residents I'd yet to meet.

"Ted, this is fantastic news," I exclaimed, uncurling myself off the couch to head back into the kitchen. "Do you think Ivan would talk to us? I told Liam to meet us at the cemetery around noon, and it would be great to ask Ivan some questions about the Whitley crypt. Ted, you just made my day!"

"I call dibs on the shower," Heidi exclaimed, jumping up from the couch in anticipation of solving the mystery of the empty crypt. I was feeling more confident by the minute that I wasn't the reason Caroline Abigail Whitley's remains were missing. "We need to make a pit stop at my place so that I can grab some clean clothes and feed my fish."

"Isn't it nice that you can just camp here whenever you want?" I was feeling better about last night's shocking find, and we'd be able to get back to what remained of the garage sale. I still had a fistful of dollar bills to spend and some small treasures to find. My good mood also had a lot to do with the fact that the hex bag I'd given to Heidi as a gift hadn't caused a dreaded zombie apocalypse. "Don't forget that we have to fit in car shopping for you sometime soon."

"Ms. Raven, I—"

"When does Beetle work again?" Heidi asked as she crossed the floor. "Maybe we can do it then."

"Ms. Raven, you need to—"

"I scheduled Beetle for working Tuesday afternoon," I replied, glancing over my shoulder to see Ted still standing next to the coffee table. He had the most peculiar look on his face, and it wasn't like him to stay around when he had plans to visit the boutique. "Ted, what's wrong?"

"I don't think it's a good idea for you to speak with Ivan, Ms. Raven."

I'd already drained my coffee cup so that I could refill it, wanting a second cup to sip on while getting ready for the day. Telling myself that my good mood wasn't about to be eviscerated, I reworded my question to get a more direct answer. Heidi had even stopped her progress to the bathroom located just behind the spiral staircase.

"Ted, why isn't it a good idea to talk with Ivan?" I asked cautiously, wondering if Ted knew more about the empty crypt than he was letting on. I made my way over to the island with an empty cup while keeping an eye on Ted. "Did he have something to do with the missing remains of Caroline Abigail Whitley?"

"Nothing like that, Ms. Raven," Ted protested, his dark gaze swinging back and forth between Heidi and me.

My heart rate began to race, and the palm of my right hand began to tingle.

Oh, this wasn't good.

Not at all.

"Don't leave me hanging, Ted," I said a little desperately, already knowing that Ted was definitely going to leave me hanging. "Why would the groundskeeper have a problem if Liam spoke to him about the Whitley family crypt?"

What groundskeeper?

Leo was back. He'd reappeared in the middle of the living room, giving his body a little shake to lose a bit of those flyaway strands.

"Ivan," I replied, turning my attention back on Ted as I set my empty coffee cup on the island to rub the palm of my hand. "Ted was just saying that he might not want to talk to us, but I don't know why."

Ivan? I don't know any Ivan. Changing the subject, I couldn't find Skippy anyway, which probably means he was the one responsible for setting up the talking raccoon gig. I've got to hand it to my nemesis. He certainly knows how to up his game.

Leo didn't know an Ivan?

Oh, my morning wasn't looking so bright anymore.

My heart was now thumping hard against my chest as I set my gaze on Ted, all but pleading with him to tell me why Leo didn't know Ivan and why said man wouldn't want to speak with me or Liam regarding the graveyard.

"Ted, who is Ivan?"

"Why, he's a reaper, Ms. Raven."

Can I have a redo on my entrance? I want a redo, Raven. Is it too much to ask that we have one normal day around here?

Chapter Six

"ARE YOU REALLY sure this is a good idea?" Heidi asked for the tenth time. She pushed her sunglasses a bit farther up the bridge of her nose, but I could still see through the tinted lenses. Her blue gaze was frantically sweeping the grounds of the graveyard like an approach radar at an airport. I'm pretty sure she was looking for any sign of Ivan. "Let's face it, Raven. You're a horrible liar. It doesn't help that I now know a reaper roams Paramour Bay waiting to collect our souls once we die."

I'm with Heidi. This is a terrible idea. Awful, in fact. We should go back home and rethink this entire approach. You know, there might be a spell in the family grimoire that erases the last twenty-four hours and any memory we have of it. Of course, with your luck, you'd end up erasing our entire existence completely... but that option is still on the table, as far as I'm concerned.

"You're not helping, Leo. And I'm sticking to the fact that I'm not responsible for our current predicament as it is, so there's no need to undo an entire day or to erase our entire existence."

It was a little bit after twelve o'clock, but I'd wanted to be early for our meeting with Liam. I'd come up with a legitimate excuse as to how Heidi and I discovered that Caroline Abigail Whitley's remains were missing. The only hitch in my plan was that I'd need to carry it out in the most believable manner. As

Heidi had so eloquently put it earlier…I was a horrible liar.

I'd struggled a lot over the fact that I couldn't share my secret with Liam. I'd blurted the truth out to Heidi. Luckily, the world hadn't ended, but I had been warned not to do it again by Leo, my mother, Aunt Rowena, the council of a coven I wasn't even a part of, and the list goes on.

Give it time. It's clear that my beloved Heidi is still digesting Ted's little revelation that our local reaper—who happens to play high-stakes poker with our Crayola, mind you—will someday pay her a visit. A reaper euphemistically named Ivan. I wonder if he chose that name? Come to think of it, I wonder what Rosemary thought of being escorted into the afterlife by a reaper named Ivan.

Maybe it was all too much, but I couldn't spend my time worrying about a reaper who I hoped I didn't meet until I was far older with a fantastic head of silver and grey hair. I was about to spin another story to the man who I was falling head over heels in love with and who made me extremely happy. In return, I lied to him often…a little too often. He was kind, compassionate, intelligent, loyal, and—I lied.

For a second, I thought you were going to say sexy. You had me halfway to regurgitating a nasty hairball onto the tip of your shoe. And just to remind you, you're wearing flats today with a purple flower instead of your usual knee-high boots. A purple flower with grooves in it so that the—well, you get the idea.

"Yeah, I get it, Leo," I replied in irritation, purposefully tucking my right foot underneath my black and purple broomstick skirt. The style was my all-time favorite, and I needed all the confidence I could get while trying to lead Liam in the right direction of a crime without revealing the truth of how I was involved. "Heidi, tell me this—should I straight up tell Liam I'm a witch?"

The answer is a rounding no. N-O. No. Do I need to repeat myself? Maybe a tattoo would help.

"Only you can answer that, doll."

Heidi patted me on the shoulder in sympathy.

Tell Heidi that I've already answered for you, in the negative.

We'd had this conversation many, many times over the last five months. I'd already exposed the supernatural realm to one human. I'd told the one secret that was meant to be kept for the safety of all supernatural beings. It hadn't been my right to do so, and I'd been left to deal with the guilt of breaking that trust. It was certainly a heavy burden, and I didn't want to add to the weight. Besides, the coven might erase me from all existence if I did it again.

Then it's simple—don't. Look at it this way. If you tell the good ol' sheriff the truth, Ivan will have several more souls to collect today—mine among them. I can only take so much stress, you know. My hair is already falling out in handfuls.

With that said, I still struggled with how I could make my relationship with Liam successful without including him in every facet of my life.

Easy. You don't tell him. Drop him like a hot rock. See? Simple.

"All I know is that I've seen the way that man looks at you, Raven. I don't think there's a thing you could tell him that would have you falling off that pedestal he's put you on."

I could always kick it out from under you. It would certainly be my pleasure.

"Showtime," Heidi said, straightening as she pushed herself off the trunk of my old Corolla. The sound of Liam's truck cut through the silence of the cemetery. "Once we hand this case off to Liam, I say we hit what is left of the garage sales and spend away our worries one dollar at a time. Besides, Ted said that he'd speak with Ivan tonight at their regular poker game. I might be having Ted inserting a few inquiries amongst the regular poker table banter. You know, how we'd really like it if we don't formally meet until we're in our nineties."

Poker. Can you believe that Ted has been playing poker with a reaper? The least they could have done was invite me to join their game. Although, now that I think about it...I wonder if Ivan is a bit peeved that I wasn't with Rosemary when he came to collect us. Remind me to ask Ted about that. I might owe Ivan a belated sympathy card or something.

Ted's announcement regarding Ivan had definitely shocked all of us. He'd never once before mentioned that he could communicate with other supernatural beings. Maybe I'd just assumed he couldn't due to his inability to hear Leo. With that said, Ted was created with the use of animation magic, which requires spells from transmutation and conjuration spheres of magic. He played such a huge part in my learning the craft, always bringing me the most amazing spell components, but this opened up many new doors.

Ted, Ted, Ted. It's all about Ted. Well, I will have you know that—

"Hi," I said softly when Liam finally stepped out of his truck. He usually wore a khaki sheriff's uniform shirt with a pair of faded blue jeans. Today, he wore a button down white dress shirt with the sleeves rolled up to his forearms. His firearm was holstered to the waistband of his jeans, and he had on his favorite brown boots. There something so charmingly handsome about the man, I could hardly stand it. And he still took my breath away every time he smiled. "I missed you last night."

"Same," Liam replied with a grin, leaning down to claim a

kiss. Even though the sun was shining and the temperature was rising, he still rubbed my arms up and down in a sign of affection. "I'm beginning to think that I can't leave you alone for one night, though. What in the world were you and Heidi doing in the graveyard last night, anyway? Hi, Heidi. You two getting into trouble as usual, huh?"

"Something like that," Heidi replied with a knowing smile. She seemed to have settled somewhat now that an armed law enforcement officer was around. I didn't want to break it to her that firearms probably did nothing to stop a reaper. "I spoke with Jack this morning, and he wanted me to tell you that you're missing all the fun."

"Three days of eight-hour lectures…I'll pass, thanks." Liam's rich laughter did nothing to ease my fears that he would see through my little white lies. "Okay. Lay it on me. What were the two of you doing in the cemetery so late last night?"

Here it goes.

I took a deep breath and said everything I'd rehearsed at least four times this morning. I could do this without a sweat, knowing that it was in the best of both our interests. Liam had a duty to protect the residents of Paramour Bay, and I had the responsibility to keep the secrets of the supernatural realm.

"It's all Leo's fault," I replied in chagrin.

Wait just a toad's ribbit. Did you just throw me under the bus again? You did, didn't you? I swear, you are the worst pet owner in the surrounding nine counties.

"Leo was chasing this squirrel, and the next moment he was gone. Heidi and I had no choice but to drive around town last night trying to find him. We were worried sick. We finally spotted him through the gates of the cemetery. Of course, we ended up parking here at the entrance and following him all the way through the graveyard to the back of the property where the crypts are lined up."

Not nice, Raven. Not nice at all. I'm going to go live with Heidi.

"First things first," Liam said, releasing his hold on me as he looked over his shoulder. I peered around him, but I didn't see anything unusual. "Is Leo safe at home?"

The second we'd heard the rumbling sound of the engine in Liam's truck, Leo had vanished. He hadn't gone far, obviously, letting me know exactly what he thought of this cover story every step of the way. Alas, it was the best I could come up with, and it would explain why we had been inside the Whitley family crypt last night.

I can see at least five holes in your story. Ten. No, make that fifteen.

"Yes, Leo is safe at home and sleeping in his favorite spot in the front windowsill."

That's exactly where I should be, but noooo. I had to be given the impossible task of making sure you acclimate to the supernatural realm. How was I supposed to know that included being sacrificed on the altar of "I can't cast a spell to save my life" on a daily basis? We're going to be taken over by zombies if you and the resident warlock keep opening portals to other planes of existence every time I turn my back.

"I'm glad to hear that Leo is safe." Liam once again peered over his shoulder, giving a slight nod of approval. What in the world was he looking for? "Ah, here's Cliff now."

Cliff?

Oh, no. This isn't good. I completely forgot about that oddball.

Who was Cliff?

A wave of worry rolled over me that there was a man named

Cliff in this scenario, and I had no idea who he was and completely afraid that his true identity might very well send me off the loony bin cliff.

Horrible pun, Raven. Just horrible.

"Who's Cliff?" Heidi asked, having no idea that Leo and I were exchanging words back and forth like a tennis match.

"Cliff Meyers," Liam responded with a quizzical glance, telling me that I should have heard of the man pulling up in a navy-blue car. It could have been a Ford, General Motors, or even a Chevrolet. It was one of those vehicles that just kind of blended together with all the other sedans—very nondescript. "He's a descendent from the Whitley family, a few times removed. You met him at the New Year's Eve bash that Oliver and Alison Bend threw at the wax museum."

I guess this wasn't such a good time for my memory loss to kick in, was it?

Had Leo been anywhere that I could have set my exasperated gaze upon him, I might have even included a pointed finger. I still couldn't recall a Cliff Meyers, but I'd met quite a few people at the New Year's Eve party. And yes, I know it's hard to believe, but Paramour Bay does have a wax museum located on the left-hand side when one drives into town. It was odd in many respects.

I'd completely forgotten that the oddball is a distant relative of Caroline Abigail Whitley. Maybe it's because he's like a wallflower and blends in wherever he goes. I mean, just look at that car.

Sure enough, I understood exactly what Leo was trying to say when a forty-some-year-old man with average features, average height, and an average smile stepped out of his average vehicle. There wasn't one distinct feature I could depict if ever asked to describe his mundane appearance. Seriously, even his clothes and shoes were as plain as brown gravy.

Serial killer.

I briefly closed my eyes at the random quip that came from Leo, because Cliff Meyers was certainly no serial killer. I was pretty sure that even Skippy could give this man a run for his money. Then again, the palm of my hand became slightly warm with the additional visitor.

See? I'm always right.

"Cliff," Liam called out, giving my hand a reassuring squeeze before taking a few steps away from me to shake Mr. Meyers' hand. "I appreciate you meeting me out here. Raven was the first to notice that something was amiss with the family crypt, so I thought we could all go take a look at it to assess the situation together. I'm well aware you come out once a month to replace the flowers and tidy up the burial chamber."

Obsessed with death…check. Maybe he prefers an icepick.

"Ms. Marigold, it's nice to see you again." Cliff shook my hand. His grip was neither firm nor soft. It was in between, fairly middle of the road. "I'm sure there's been a misunderstanding regarding Great-Grandmother Carolyn's stone coffin."

An unhealthy attachment to centuries long-dead relatives…check. Maybe a candlestick…in the crypt…with Colonel Mustard.

I forced a smile, wondering who in their right mind called a woman centuries old *great grandmother*. Cliff walked past me to greet Heidi before rocking back on the worn heels of his brown loafers. I never would have noticed that the movement was a nervous gesture had Cliff not glanced at his watch with a bit of anxious worry.

Wants to avoid the scene of the crime…check. I've changed my mind. A rope. Definitely a rope.

"Cliff's not a bad guy, if you give him a chance," Liam murmured once we began walking through the rusted gates of the cemetery. Cliff led the way, which was actually rather surprising. Heidi had fallen into step behind him, no doubt with Leo somewhere by her side. Liam and I pulled up the rear, giving us the privacy to talk as we walked. "He's the mortician in town, and he doesn't get out a lot. With that said, he's a darn fine poker player."

Check! Check! Check! Holy cow, did I hit this one on the head or what?

Leo had begun his mantra at the word mortician, but someone had to do it, right? Cliff's career choice did not make him a serial killer.

I bet Cliff keeps Ivan busy with all those dead bodies. I see your dead body and raise you one soul.

"Liam, I'm not so sure it was a good idea to call Mr. Meyers before seeing the Whitley crypt yourself." I could feel the weight of Liam's gaze on my face as I sidestepped a divot, grateful when he pressed his right hand against my lower back. The warmth of his touch through my blouse gave me the strength to blurt out the rest of my story. "Mrs. Whitley's stone coffin is completely empty."

The good ol' sheriff looks like he caught a glimpse of Ivan. I'm not sure if I've ever seen someone lose color in their face quite that fast. Can you imagine his reaction if he ever did meet Ivan, a teetotaling ghost, or a soul-eating ghoul? Just food for thought.

Leo sounded as if he were hacking up that hairball he'd mentioned earlier, but that was the cackle of his laugh.

Soul-eating ghoul? Food for thought? Get it?

It didn't come as much of a surprise when Liam quickly stepped in front of me to stop our progress. His shocked expression pretty much told me that maybe I should have dropped that itty-bitty fact over the phone. His reaction had nothing to do with the supernatural and everything to do with me not disclosing all the details of the potential crime scene.

Speaking of potential, have you spoken to Rye? At least he accepts his flaws and is willing to make amends.

"Raven, you only said that the old wooden doors to the crypt seemed to have been pried open and that it appeared as if the stone lid had been shifted a bit," Liam reiterated what we'd spoken about this morning, but his eyes darkened in astonishment. "You never said a word about an empty coffin or a missing corpse."

The good ol' sheriff has you there, Raven.

"I know, but I didn't think you'd call in a family member," I said, waving my hand in exasperation toward the direction that Cliff and Heidi were taking across the grounds of the cemetery. "I didn't even realize that any Whitleys were still in the area. Well, besides Arthur Whitley."

The recluse. Between the mortician and the recluse, I'm wondering if this family might be harboring some psychotic tendencies.

"Let's keep walking while you tell me everything you know," Liam exclaimed with a sigh and that same sideways glance of curiosity he'd been giving me for a while now.

A part of me wondered if he didn't sense something was different about me, but he'd never come straight out and asked for answers to some of the peculiar events around town.

You mean the fact that three people have been murdered since you've come to town or the alarming detail that none of your stories make any sense?

Leo was exaggerating.

Let's see...there was the warlock trying to steal the family gri-

moire whose body you found in the back of the tea shop, the state-appointed tax auditor gentleman who bit the dust over at the inn, and the carnival worker who was murdered by an evil clown. Did I miss any?

Okay, Leo might have a miniscule point.

Let's not forget we also had an arsonist in our midst. Then there was the missing wax figure from the wax museum…you know, the one who just happens to resemble Ted.

Leo was making the mysteries around Paramour Bay sound worse than they really were, because there had been extenuating circumstances in all of those situations. Liam had taken the crimes in stride and had even made multiple arrests.

"As I said, Heidi and I were looking for Leo when we saw him run through the graveyard." I slipped my hands inside the pockets of my skirt, still noticing the warm spot in the center of my palm. It had to be Cliff Meyer's presence, right? On second thought, it could be due to the sapphire ring I'd put for safekeeping in my right pocket. "The doors were open, and we thought that maybe Leo had gone inside. We were a bit scared, but we searched the crypt anyway and saw the lid on the coffin had been moved. We had a peek inside thinking…"

I'm not quite sure any sane person would have looked inside a coffin while being inside a dark crypt at night. It was a struggle to come up with an excuse that didn't sound as though we were—

Grave robbers? Ghost hunters? Thrill seekers? I can come up with more titles if you'd like, but it's all downhill from there.

"You thought that Leo might have been trapped inside," Liam finished with a nod of approval. "You love him. I get it. I would have done the same thing."

That excuse was so not on my list.

"We did think that Leo might have been inside," I replied, grabbing onto the life preserver Liam had just thrown me. "Which is why I called you this morning to check out the crypt in case we were wrong. It was dark, we were a bit uneasy being inside the crypt that late at night, and we could have easily been mistaken."

Not a bad recovery. Now all we have to do is make sure Ivan doesn't make an appearance. One would think he would have showed himself last night to let us know what happened to Caroline Abigail Whitley's remains. Then again, no one died. Ted really needs to track down Ivan and get to the bottom of what happened here. I wonder if Skippy and his friends are in league with Ivan. It would certainly explain how he managed to get a raccoon to talk. Having a reaper in one's back pocket is very clever indeed.

"Well, I'll have Cliff stay behind with you and Heidi while I check things over." Liam was focused on the numerous crypts ahead, and I noted they weren't as eerie as they had been last night. It was amazing how the warm sunlight could alter one's perspective. "You know, you could have called me last night when Leo went missing. I would have helped you search for him."

I'm not sure how I feel about this, Raven. The good ol' sheriff is showing affection toward me, and I've shown him nothing but disdain. Make it stop.

"I didn't want to bother you while you were meeting with the town council." For the first time this morning, I hadn't smudged the truth. I wanted this moment to last a little longer, so I asked a question that would guarantee a normal conversation. "How did it go, anyway?"

A change of subject is good. I don't do affection. Well, unless it comes from Heidi or I've consumed copious amounts of catnip...then anyone can rub my belly. All bets are off.

"Let's just say the emergency town council meeting was a front to get people over for a game of poker," Liam said with a fond smile, having gotten used to how Mayor Sanders worked when his wife was out of town. "I wouldn't have minded a call from you, let's put it that way. You would have saved me a hundred bucks and a budget reduction."

You know, a hundred bucks could buy a lot of catnip. I realize they don't know I can play poker, but I'm beginning to feel unwanted...two poker home games and no invites.

We'd reached the crypt, but there was a peaceful vibe over the graveyard that hadn't been there last night. Heidi and Cliff were talking about the mortuary's taxes, and she'd somehow gotten him to relax somewhat with her reassurance that she would do just as good of a job as Beetle had done with his business.

"Cliff, why don't you let me take a look first?" Liam suggested in such a manner that no one would have ever thought he'd done it with a specific objective in mind. He certainly was good at his job, and another doubt flittered through my thoughts that maybe he knew more about me than he was letting on. "I'll be right back."

Liam had nonchalantly rubbed his fingers across mine when I'd removed my hand from my pocket. I realized that the energy coiling in my palm remained steady, reassuring me that he wasn't walking into something dangerous. With that said, my inherent sense hadn't helped us in the least last night.

There also wasn't a soul-eating ghoul in the crypt at that time.

True. I didn't get a sense that one was inside the burial chamber now, either.

I never entertained the thought, but maybe Ivan cleaned up your spell-flubbing mess. He wouldn't appreciate a soul-eating ghoul in his territory, you know.

Heidi continued to talk with Cliff, keeping him occupied while we waited for word from Liam. He'd see that the crypt was empty, the infamous ring was missing, along with whatever treasures that might have been buried with Caroline Abigail Whitley.

You know, I could totally get on board with the whole non-supernatural blame game if it wasn't for one thing.

I couldn't tear away my gaze from Liam inspecting the doors, though he didn't say a word as he finally stepped inside. He'd unclipped his flashlight from his utility belt, eventually disappearing into the darkness with the exception of a faded beam.

The raccoon. A talking raccoon. That is not an everyday occurrence, Raven. That's not to say having Ivan on our side doesn't work in our favor, because it does. I do feel for the reaper, though. He's probably out there right now trying to corral that masked garbage eater by himself.

Leo must have sunk into a quiet introspection about why he'd envisioned a talking raccoon or he was convincing himself that Ivan was truly hunting the poor little furbaby. Even Heidi and Cliff waited for any sound to indicate that we should either go inside or wait for Liam to exit. Five seconds turned into ten. Ten into fifteen.

It does make you wonder if your danger radar is on the fritz, doesn't it? For all we know, Caroline Abigail Whitley actually did turn into some soul-eating ghoul and is currently sucking down the good ol' sheriff with a supernatural straw. I'm sure reapers get days off. Wouldn't you think?

I couldn't take this waiting any longer, so I took a step forward and had every intention of calling out to Liam when we all jumped back in fright at something large, black, and white hurtling out of the darkness.

Rabid raccoon! Run for your lives!

Chapter Seven

I'M NOT GOING to sugarcoat it. *That went better than anyone had a right to expect.*

"Leo, you did your disappearing act right in front of Cliff Meyers," I said in disbelief, slowing maneuvering my beat-up old Corolla into the driveway of one Arthur Whitley. "How is that better than I could have expected? I'm pretty sure he's going to need psychiatric counseling after today."

Oh, trust me. That man needed counseling way before a raccoon landed on his face. Did you see that flying back kick? The MMA hasn't got anything on that masked bandit. Mr. Talking Garbage Disposal could give Skippy a run for his money in the ninja training department. Bottom line was that you now know I was telling the truth.

"Leo, it was a normal everyday raccoon," I reminded Leo for the tenth time. "The scared little critter didn't utter one word before he was sent scurrying away in fright. I think we scared him half to death, poor little guy."

You keep telling yourself that, missy. They carry all kinds of nasty diseases, like the Black Plague and Ebola. I hate having to do all the heavy lifting around here, but I seem to have no choice—I'm going raccoon hunting.

"That's not a good idea, Leo. Raccoons can do a lot of damage to an average housecat. You might not fare too well," I cautioned, not immediately turning off the engine as I took in my surroundings. I was feeling quite out of place in this upscale neighborhood of waterfront properties. I'd counted more than a few BMWs, a top-end Lexus, and a couple of those luxury class Mercedes in the various driveways. Sure, my cottage had the perfect view of the bay, but I was on the wrong end of town away from all the ritzy houses. "The last thing we need for you to do is get bit by a rabid raccoon. Leave the poor thing alone, okay? Leo? Leo?"

I should have known he wouldn't take my advice, and now I had to go speak with an elderly recluse about his great-great-great-great grandmother's missing corpse. I'm not even sure that was the correct number of greats. I was horrible at math, and Caroline Abigail Whitley had died many, many years ago.

As a matter of fact, it was about the same time as the witch trials in Connecticut were kicking off. That was a decidedly dangerous time for my kind.

I'm pretty sure that Leo also thought this afternoon had gone better than expected due to the fact that Liam had declared the crypt secure—meaning that no foul play had been committed outside of someone breaking in. Trust me, his declaration had practically done to me what the raccoon had done to Cliff Meyers.

Either way, I had to go down inside the burial chamber to see for myself.

Sure enough, the crypt had been secured after our earlier encounter.

No sign of tampering with the contents had been detected.

After having Liam take us back down in the crypt and seeing that the lid of the stone coffin had been put back in its rightful place, we'd had no choice but to accept that nothing seemed out of turn inside the burial chamber. Cliff Meyers became more talkative after that, saying that midnight strolls through the graveyard might cause people to see things that weren't actually there—though that definitely wasn't the case in our situation.

Unfortunately, it wasn't like I could fess up that I had Caroline Abigail Whitley's ring in my pocket. I'd left that part of the story out when I'd given my explanation to Liam.

You see?

That was the problem with lying—one could never keep their facts in order and there were too many strings to be pulled once you started.

Heidi and I had ended up looking like two hapless females who'd overreacted to the nightly ambiance of a graveyard. I'm not going to say it hadn't burned my pride, because it did…and there wasn't a thing we could do about it now.

Well, there was, but Liam had no clue I was taking a little side trip.

Don't get me wrong.

The second Heidi and I had gotten to the car, I'd quickly called Rye and practically pleaded with him to tell me that he'd gone back to the crypt to clean things up and close the coffin. Needless to say, he didn't alleviate my fears. He assured me that he hadn't gone back to the crypt and made it look as if nothing had happened last night.

I did briefly consider that Ivan might have fixed everything the way Leo had suggested, but a reaper's job was to collect souls…not to clean up after a crime.

Heidi and I had no choice but to come up with a plan, so I'd dropped her back off at the cottage so that she could begin looking through the family grimoire for a spell I could use on the ring in order to find out how it had ended up at a garage sale for a measly fifty cents. While she was doing my magical research, I was going to pay a visit to Arthur Whitley under the apologetic pretense of what had occurred at the family crypt. Maybe he had some insight into what happened there.

Of course, I was really going to see if the palm of my hand became sensitive to the presence of the elderly recluse. If Mr. Whitley had ill intentions and was somehow responsible for the missing remains of his ancestor, then I'd rather be given a forewarning before choosing the proper spell to deliver the woman back to her final resting place.

Something caught my attention.

At first, I thought it was sunlight glaring off the front window. It took me a moment to realize that the white doily patterned curtain was being moved by someone standing just out of sight. Well, it was turning out that Ted was right about Mr. Whitley being a bit of a paranoid type. Then again, I'd be rather curious to see who had pulled into my driveway, too.

I flashed him a smile and gave him a reassuring wave, but all that did was cause him to drop the curtain quickly back into place. It didn't take me long to shut off my engine and open my car door, not bothering to roll up the window or lock the door behind me. I was only going to be a minute or two, and it was broad daylight in the middle of a rather wealthy neighborhood. The last car anyone would want to steal was mine.

It struck me as I walked up the small path to Mr. Whitley's front door that I could literally hear the soothing sounds of the bay. The ambiance was very peaceful. The mournful horns of the cargo ships carried over the light breeze, and turning my head just right allowed me to catch the cry of the seagulls soaring over the shore headlong into the breeze.

I didn't have such a scene setting at the cottage, most likely because I was farther away from the marinas and the other disturbances. The view from the back of the property must be absolutely stunning. Mine was similar, but with more of the natural trees blocking a clear view.

I also noted that Arthur Whitley kept an absolutely pristine yard, with the edging just so with each blade of grass trimmed to perfection and greener than an emerald. The random thought of emeralds practically made the sapphire ring in my skirt pocket burn a hole through the fabric, and the phantom heat against my thigh had me quickening my pace up the small walk and ringing the doorbell in haste.

Mr. Whitley couldn't have been more than eight steps away from the front door near the window, but I pressed the button once more when almost a minute had passed and no one had answered the audible chime.

Was Mr. Whitley really going to ignore someone at his front door, knowing full well I'd seen him looking out the window earlier? I guess I didn't blame him. I'd done the same before, though that was when I had lived in the city along with the convenience of a peephole. I didn't get many visitors at the cottage. Then again, no one in their right mind would randomly pull up the gravel drive to what appeared to be a haunted house. Nan hadn't been big on curb appeal.

Right when I was about to give up, the deadbolt on the door gave way. Then another…and then a third.

Just how many locks did Arthur Whitley have on the front entrance of his house?

The door finally cracked open, only to come to an abrupt stop courtesy of a telltale gold chain. Arthur Whitley's weathered features were barely detectable, but one of his bushy white eyebrows could be seen as clear as day.

"What do you want?"

Paranoid and odd weren't the only adjectives I would have used to describe Arthur Whitley. Rude ranked right up there in the top ten, but it wasn't so much his question that had me tacking on the word than the tone he'd used.

"Hi, Mr. Whitley. My name is…"

"I asked you a question, young lady. What do you want?"

So much for proper introductions.

"I was hoping to speak with you about something that happened inside your family crypt at the graveyard." I held my breath as I laced my fingers together in hopes I'd get some type of reaction in the palm of my hand. So far, my skin only maintained the tingling sensation that had begun to form last night. "Actually, I've come to apologize for stirring things up."

I waited for Mr. Whitley to make a decision, fully expecting to have the door slammed shut in my face. Surprisingly, he gently closed the beautifully ornate wooden door after a slight nod of concession. I could easily hear the scrape of the chain being undone before the sight of a gorgeous tiled entryway appeared before me.

"Well, what are you waiting for?" Mr. Whitley asked in a gruff manner, using his cane to quickly usher me inside. "Get in here, already. You're letting out all the cool air."

"Of course," I exclaimed, rushing forward before the elderly man changed his mind. I'm not sure what I expected—maybe a hoarder's paradise with newspapers piled high and knickknacks covered with dust. It wasn't really nice to prejudge others, but that's the image that appeared in my mind when thinking about a recluse. "Mr. Whitley, you have a very beautiful home."

It was hard not to admire the various vases and paintings that were set and hung specifically to catch the eye of an admirer.

The knickknacks I had been expecting were more in line with small statues and unique antiques that must have been in the family for generations upon generations. A floral fabric covered the formal living room's furniture, and the white lace doily curtains were spotless.

Was that gingerbread I smelled?

Mr. Whitley squinted as he took in my appearance, causing his bushy grey eyebrows to form a perfect V. He twisted his mouth in thoughtfulness before nodding in approval. I wasn't sure what he had based his approval on, but it was better than being kicked to the curb before getting the answers I sought.

"Thank you for speaking with me, Mr. Whitley," I began with a small smile of appreciation. I wasn't sure he saw it when he walked past me to enter the formal living room. "You see, my cat ran into the cemetery last night and—"

I stopped talking when I heard the click of a woman's shoes coming from the hallway that no doubt led to the back of the house. I'm not sure why I thought Mr. Whitley lived alone, but again the image of a recluse didn't include a spouse. Besides, Ted and Leo didn't mention a female companion.

"Arthur? Who was at the door? I've told those children from down the block numerous times that—" A woman in what I would guess was her late sixties finally appeared, wearing an apron and wiping her hands on a dishtowel. She came up short when she caught sight of me. A stern frown appeared on her rather rigid features about the same time the palm of my hand began to harness energy. "Just who are you, miss, and what is it that you want?"

"Now, now, Stella," Mr. Whitley muttered in pacification as he continued to shuffle his well-worn brown dress shoes across the hardwood floor and then the oriental rug. He didn't stop to take a seat as I'd expected him to, but instead it seemed as if he was walking to the antique bookcase on the other side of the room. "Ms. Marigold is my guest. Please treat her as such. I'm sure she'd like a hot cup of tea and some of those cookies you've been baking all morning."

Ms. Stella continued to glare at me as if I'd been the rude one, but she eventually left and headed back to the kitchen. Two things struck me, though the latter was more of a shocking revelation. Ms. Stella was some type of housekeeper or cook, and I'd never fully introduced myself.

"Mr. Whitley, how did you know my name?"

Ms. Stella might have gone back into the kitchen, but the energy coiling in the palm of my hand remained. Was it due to Arthur Whitley's mention of my last name or his housekeeper? He'd clearly known who I was before I even got out of my car.

"Anyone with working eyes can see that you're related to Rosemary Marigold." Mr. Whitley was now standing in front of the antique bookcase. He'd rested his cane against his hip as he began searching for a book. "Now, continue with your story about your wayward cat."

Arthur Whitley had known my grandmother?

I mean, I guess it would stand to reason that the two of them would have crossed paths. I know that Ted and Leo mentioned that the Whitleys didn't often come into town and preferred to do their shopping in the city, but I'm sure there had been some exceptions when he was younger and more mobile.

"Well," I began once more, clearing my throat, "my friend and I chased after my cat, who had somehow gained entrance into your family's crypt. It seems that someone had recently pried open the heavy wooden doors. I'm so sorry, but I went inside to make sure he hadn't gotten lost somewhere. I know this is going to sound crazy, but we…well, we truly believed at the time that the lid on Caroline Abigail Whitley's coffin had been moved to the side."

Mr. Whitley's weathered hand hesitated over the line of books above him for a brief moment. I'm not sure what reaction I expected to hearing my story about the possibility that someone might have desecrated his family's burial chambers, but this wasn't it.

"I informed Sheriff Liam Drake of what we thought had happened, and he called a gentleman by the name of Cliff Meyers to come take a look."

"Clifford." Mr. Whitley said the name in an offended huff, telling me that the two men didn't quite see eye to eye. He'd gone back to looking for a specific book that appeared to remain elusive to his aging eyes. "There's always a black sheep in every family. Who wants to spend their days and nights dealing with dead people? There's a reason we Whitleys own so much real estate and marinas, and that's to continue to grow the family fortune for the generations that will come after us. Clifford just had to be out of the ordinary, not that he achieved that dubious distinction. Oh, my poor sister must be rolling in her grave."

Liam had taken the time to look over the other vaults in the Whitley family crypt, but I wondered if Heidi and I shouldn't go back some time tonight and take another look. Something was going on in that graveyard, and I needed to make sure it was being done by unscrupulous humans and not anything Rye or I had done by opening up some extraplanar portal to another existence.

"Fortunately, there was nothing visibly wrong with crypt when we went back there this morning," I informed him, waiting for some reaction that would let me know if he'd had something to do with the desecration of a resting place of his own relative. "I realize that Mr. Meyers is the one who takes care of the family crypt, but I thought you should know what was going on. And I truly apologize for any confusion I may have caused when I called Liam to—"

"Confusion?" Mr. Whitley asked, looking over his shoulder at me with obvious displeasure at my word selection. He clicked his tongue and turned back to his task of finding whatever it was he was looking for, finally setting a knotted index finger on top of a dark brown leather-bound book that had seen better days. He slid it from its spot before grabbing his cane and turning to face me. "There was no confusion, Ms. Marigold. Your grandmother warned me this would happen, so I've been keeping an eye on the family crypt for the last eight or nine months without that nincompoop Clifford any the wiser. He's an imbecile."

Mr. Whitley began to make his way forward, his cane in one hand and the leather-bound book in the other. I was still trying to digest the shocking announcement that he'd not only known my grandmother, but that she'd warned him of something happening in the crypt.

Nan hadn't been psychic, as far as I knew.

Then again, this new life I'd been handed was nothing but one long line of alarming discoveries after another.

"What did my Nan warn you about, Mr. Whitley?" I asked cautiously, making a note that the heat coiled in the palm of my hand hadn't lessened one bit since Ms. Stella had left the room. I had an innate sense that the danger I was sensing came from the book Mr. Whitley was currently holding out to me in offering. "Did she say that the remains of your ancestor would go missing?"

Of course, what I really wanted to ask Mr. Whitley was if he knew my grandmother was a witch. Had Nan exposed herself and our lineage to one of the founding families? If so…this changed nearly everything.

Chapter Eight

WHY WOULD YOU even think such a thing? *Of course, good ol' Arthur doesn't know anything about your grandmother or your family secret. On to more pressing news...the garbage eater wasn't anywhere to be found. I did run into Skippy, though. He acted like today was any other day, so I'm amending the Skippy involvement theory to naught.*

Leo's return came not a moment too soon, and thankfully remained invisible. Hopefully, he had some insight on what Mr. Whitley could possibly be talking about.

Insight? He's an old geezer with more money than he can possibly spend in his last few years on this earth. I wonder if he has a date with good ol' Ivan any time soon.

"Your grandmother was deeply involved with holistic medicine, young lady." Mr. Whitley once more nudged the book toward me, which I had no choice but to take. The dark brown leather was cool to the touch, and the pages were outlined in gold trim. The odd thing about the timeworn book was that there was no title. I carefully turned it over, but once again...nothing. "So was my wife, but it was my mother who got my sweet Rosalyn into holistic remedies, who learned from her mother and so on."

Don't overreact. The Whitleys were literally into nature's storehouse of home remedies, which nowadays is referred to as holistic medicine. Nine or ten years ago when Mr. Whitley's wife was still alive, she was a frequent visitor at the tea shop. Hey, would you look at that? My memory is quite keen today, isn't it? I'm telling you, that shipment from Honduras has medicinal properties to it that sharpen the senses.

Those tink, tink, tink clicks on the tiled floor began once more, and I tensed as Ms. Stella walked stiffly into the living room with a tray in hand. There was a bone china tea set hand-painted with what had to be twenty-four carat gold gilt. It was magnificent. That particular set definitely didn't come from a shelf in my shop, along with its matching plate piled high with those gingerbread cookies I'd caught the delicious scent of when first entering the house.

Wow. Would you look at that face? She's the definition of resting b—

"Those cookies smell delicious, Ms. Stella," I said quickly, more so to cut Leo off before he said something that might invite negative karma. "Thank you so much."

Ms. Stella only gave one nod in recognition of my appreciation. She was too busy setting the tray on the coffee table while shooting glaring daggers at Mr. Whitley. I bet the housekeeper had been with the Whitleys for a while and probably knew quite a bit about the family history. It was more than apparent she didn't approve of her employer talking to me today, or any other day for that matter.

I remember her now. I never did like that old bat. I wonder if I slip Ivan a few extra chips if he would—

"Would it be too much trouble to ask for cream?" I inquired, really wishing Leo would stop beckoning karma as if she were just another flight attendant refilling our drinks.

I'm sure karma was pretty busy with that raccoon for landing on good ol' Cliff's face before performing that jaw-breaking back kick. I wonder if karma is open to a bribe or two.

Ms. Stella lifted her right eyebrow, which was drawn on with a light brown eyebrow pencil. She then pointed toward the small cream bowl right next to the one containing sugar cubes. It was easy to decipher that I'd offended her by believing she'd be neglectful in her duties.

Now who's the one offending people?

"Thank you, Stella," Mr. Whitley said dismissively with a wave of his hand. I was beginning to understand why the housekeeper had such a stern demeanor. It couldn't have been easy working for a man like him. "Now leave us, please, so that I can fill Ms. Marigold in on what really happened at the cemetery earlier this morning."

Something other than what you witnessed happen at the cemetery earlier this morning? Raven, I clearly missed most of this conversation. I must say that I don't care for the direction this is going. Put the book down. You know, sometimes it's better to be left in the dark than to know the truth.

Ms. Stella parted her thin lips before imparting a huff of frustration. She quietly, though with much displeasure, turned and left the room. I didn't want to be kept in the dark, especially if there was something about Nan that could help me figure out why the remains of Caroline Abigail Whitley went missing...only to be returned.

Well, we don't exactly know that her remains have been returned. We only know that someone put the crypt back together—ohhhhh. Now I'm starting to see the whole picture.

"Where were we?" Mr. Whitley asked, scratching his head as he slowly made his way to one of the formal chairs in front of the coffee table. He took a seat without a groan, leaning his cane against the arm of the seat. "Come on, now. Sit. What are you waiting for, young lady?"

"I'm waiting for you properly to answer me, Mr. Whitley," I responded directly, clearly seeing the same mental picture that Leo was and coming to the same conclusion. "Why were you at the cemetery this morning? Did you reseal your great-great-great-great grandmother's coffin with that stone lid?"

I'd seen how much strength it had taken Rye to shift the stone lid in order to get a better look inside, and there was absolutely no way that Arthur Whitley alone could have put it back in place.

Not unless he had help. Wait just a frog's hop. You don't suppose that the garbage eater belongs to Arthur Whitley, do you? I've changed my mind, Raven. Look inside the book. Is it full of necromancy spells? I wouldn't put it past these Whitleys to create their own army of undead zombies.

I was too busy watching as Mr. Whitley began pouring both of us tea with a somewhat trembling hand due to age, though he didn't let that stop him. It wasn't long before he sat back with a cup of tea and a cookie. Trust me, he didn't strike me as the cookie eating kind of elderly man, either. I was beginning to accept that not all things were as they seemed.

Exactly. Like the talking raccoon. Look inside that book, Raven, and see if the Whitleys weren't dabbling in something dark that they had no right to be fiddling with. I wouldn't put it past these bumbling fools to have stumbled upon an ancient magical tome.

I wish it had been something that simple, but I'm pretty sure that the reason my palm had begun harvesting energy was to warn about the bombshell Mr. Whitley was about to drop right in the middle of this formal living room.

You make it sound like he's about to push the big red button for a nuclear launch. Whatever he has to say can't be as bad as you and Rye opening portals to the afterlife through some convoluted magical mishap.

"My dear Ms. Marigold, I most certainly was at the cemetery earlier this morning. It was also me and Stella who were able to put things back to where they belong, though it sucked the energy right out of us doing so," Mr. Whitley explained calmly after taking a sip of his tea while leaving me still standing in shock at his admission. "Unfortunately, the two of us putting things in their rightful place didn't include Caroline Abigail's remains. Do you know where they might have gotten off to, Ms. Marigold?"

It doesn't quite rival a nuclear explosion, but the old geezer has definitely blown my mind.

"Of course not. I haven't any idea," I replied in haste, having an inkling of suspicion that I would find my answers faster if I opened the book I currently had in my grasp. I also didn't want Mr. Whitley to think my visit here today had anything to do with guilt. "Why would you believe I had something to do with the desecration of one of your family's final resting place?"

"I've been on this earth for a very long time, Ms. Marigold." Mr. Whitley nodded toward the leather-bound book I had clutched in my hands. He took his time savoring another sip of tea and then taking a bite of his gingerbread cookie. Only when he nodded his approval at the delicious taste did he finish explaining what he'd meant. "Stella and I had no choice but to make things appear normal once we realized what had taken place. We took care of what needed to be done."

What does good ol' Arthur mean by that, Raven? We took care of what needed to be done...that last sentence sounded a bit ominous, don't you think? This is taking way too long. The suspense is killing me, and that's not fair to Skippy or that garbage eater.

"Why would you actively cover up a crime, Mr. Whitley?" I asked cautiously, finally reaching for the cover of the leather-bound book. Leo wasn't the only impatient one, and Mr. Whitley was taking too long by drinking his tea and eating his cookie. "Liam thought my friend and I overreacted last night due to the circumstances, and now there is no evidence to the contrary."

Mr. Whitley slowly nodded as if what I'd said made sense to him. Even so, he took another bite of the gingerbread cookie as he continued to regard me...suspiciously. I'd been nothing but honest with him, yet his sharp blueish-green eyes told me he didn't believe a word I'd said since entering his home. Did he have some special insight that I wasn't aware of?

How does it feel to be the other shoe?

Leo had totally botched that old saying, but I got his meaning. I hadn't believed him about the talking raccoon, and now here I was being doubted by Mr. Whitley.

No, it wasn't nice.

What did Mr. Whitley know that we didn't?

The answer lies in the book. Wow. I'm like an old wise mentor from those feel good movies.

I ever so slowly pulled back the front cover of the book, the leather spine crackling from being unused for so long. At first, I wasn't sure what I was looking at until I used the silk bookmark to turn to the page that had been purposefully saved. I began to read the content more thoroughly, and it wasn't long before my heart began to race once more and a cold sweat broke out onto my skin.

No wonder the palm of my hand had harnessed energy in an attempt to protect me...and the town of Paramour Bay by extension.

Protect Paramour Bay? What did you find, Raven? Was I right about the raccoon apocalypse? I was, wasn't I?

"Ms. Marigold, that book you hold in your hand is the secret to youth." Mr. Whitley took another bite of his gingerbread cookie as if he hadn't just announced what could possibly expose the supernatural realm to the rest of the world. "It's been exactly three hundred and eighty years since my great-great-great-great grandmother took a very special sapphire ring to the grave with her…the exact length of time needed for that precious gem to harness the energy of the earth in order to provide eternal youth for one of her descendants."

Would you look at that? You were spot on with the number of greats.

Being right about the amount of generations that had passed gave me no comfort when a spell of this magnitude was about to be unleashed from the grave—by a mere human.

Well, when you put it like that…

Chapter Nine

"JACK IS ON his way here now from the airport," Heidi said
with reluctance, having already pulled the phone away from
her ear and disconnected the call. Her blue eyes were filled with
worry, but I wasn't about to concern her even more by divulging
my theories. It was fortunate she hadn't asked me point blank
what I was considering doing. Otherwise, she would have known
immediately I was hatching something and cancelled her plans.
In turn, her abrupt decision to cancel would have made Jack
suspicious. "Are you sure you don't want me to hang around?"

*My dear Heidi has a point. She might be helpful in this situa-
tion.*

Leo was just saying that because he was a wee bit jealous and
despised the fact that Heidi was dating a detective.

*Oh, trust me…that oaf of a detective could be an archangel for
all I care. He still wouldn't be good enough for my Heidi.*

The point I was trying to make originally was that I wasn't
so sure Heidi should cancel her plans, and I wasn't about to ruin
her Saturday night with this tomfoolery.

You see, I'd come back to the cottage directly after I'd finished speaking with Mr. Whitley. His claim that someone in his
family had unearthed the sapphire ring to attain eternal youth
had been said with complete conviction, which could only mean
one thing—he had no idea that I was in possession of said

precious gem.

Don't get me wrong.

He out and out accused me of being the one to take the sapphire ring, but he didn't know for sure, especially after my unexpected visit…and that was to my benefit.

Mr. Whitley had continued to enjoy his tea and cookies while casually explaining that he'd rigged the crypt with a single security camera so that he could keep an eye on the family secret from the privacy of his residence. At no point did he offer any apologies for what he'd done. Then again, if he were telling the truth…well, he'd only been doing what he'd thought was the best course of action at the time.

As for Clifford Meyers, he had no clue of what his older uncle had done. He was completely in the dark. Still, who else would have known about the security feature? It was that sole camera that had alerted Mr. Whitley that someone had desecrated the grave. An alarm had been triggered, causing Mr. Whitley and Stella to realize something had occurred at the cemetery last night. Unfortunately, it was to find that the camera had been damaged.

The footage only showed static, meaning that the assailant had known all along there had been a security camera installed inside the crypt. Mr. Whitley had assured me that no one outside of him and Stella had known about the camera's existence, but obviously he had been wrong.

It was also his way of being very passive-aggressive, indicating that I could have had something to do with the family's missing ring and the desecration of the Whitley's crypt. After carefully navigating that conversation, it was then that I realized he truly didn't know anything about my family secret. His wife had spoken to my grandmother about the book she'd found amongst some rather old books in the family library. It hadn't taken Mr. Whitley's wife long to seek out the person most likely to know about holistic means.

Bottom line?

Mr. Whitley believed that Nan had told me all about the powers the sapphire ring contained and that it was buried with Caroline Abigail Whitley. He'd basically accused me of raiding her crypt without ever actually verbalizing his accusation.

He then took the book from my practically burning hand and all but told me the ring would be useless without the spell. I'm pretty sure there was an underlying threat to his tone that indicated he'd burn the book before allowing anyone other than him to obtain immortality.

Oddly enough, I think that was Mr. Whitley's way of saying I should come clean and we could come to some sort of agreement. It was nothing short of bribery, but I'd stuck to my guns and my claim that I had no idea what he was talking about.

Can a person burn a sapphire? That would solve all of our problems.

"Heidi, you deserve a nice evening with Jack," I said, meaning every word. I'd taken so long to answer that she'd even held her phone up to indicate all she had to do was call Jack back to cancel their plans. "I promise to text you if I find anything of substance in my research of this so-called claim of eternal youth. You and I both know that all kinds of folktales exist. The idea of an enchanted gem harvesting magical energy for three hundred and eighty years and then it being used in some type of ritual to bestow immortality on a human is next to nil."

I'd already made a pot of coffee, even though it was only four o'clock in the afternoon. Having gone by the tea shop to check on Beetle, I'd picked up a fresh grind of Columbian Supremo, and he'd offered to close up at five o'clock since he was driving into the city to meet my mother for dinner. That was another story altogether that I didn't even want to think about—my mother dating my part-time employee at the shop.

Hairball.

I completely reciprocated Leo's stomach-churning nausea at the litany of disturbing images that thought produced.

"Liam is coming over in a few hours, which gives me just enough time to research the history of the Whitley family here in Paramour Bay and to find out if there is any truth to Mr. Whitley's claims. If Mr. Meyers sees himself as some sort of guardian of the family crypt, then it would be a safe bet that Clifford was the one who desecrated the Whitley's burial chambers in search of valuables."

"Cliff *was* acting more than a bit odd this morning," Heidi pointed out before walking to the window. She stroked Leo's back while making sure Jack hadn't pulled up out front. "I still don't understand how such an expensive ring ended up in a basket with costume jewelry at a garage sale."

If the oddball thought it was his responsibility to guard the family crypt, then maybe he was the one to chuck the ring into a random basket. Maybe he didn't want his old geezer of an uncle to get his grubby hands on it. Such a decision would solve everyone's problems, right?

"Jack is here," Heidi called out, leaning down to give Leo a kiss on the head. "Be good, my handsome boy. And make sure Raven stays out of trouble."

Please tell my beloved Heidi that the odds are against me in accomplishing that feat.

"Call or text me if anything happens!"

Heidi was gone in a blink of an eye, leaving me sitting on

one of the stools at the island while I thought over our predicament. I took a sip of my coffee, allowing the rich warmth to flow through me and the caffeine to do its job.

"You make an excellent point, Leo."

I do? I mean, of course, I do. Just refresh my memory on what that exact point was again.

"You said that Mr. Meyers tossing away the ring would solve his problems of having to watch the crypt. Doing so would definitely help him in his quest, so maybe he *was* the one who dropped the ring into a basket of costume jewelry. No one would ever be the wiser, and anyone looking for the sapphire ring would eventually give up their search once they found that the ring was no longer buried with Caroline Abigail Whitley."

Why not just ask the oddball? Then we wouldn't have to be sitting here wondering who tossed the ring away as if it was nothing more than a piece of cheap costume jewelry. I do have the rest of my Honduras blend to get to, and the remainder of my Saturday night is still salvageable.

"What if someone tried to harness the ring's supposed power, but he or she had no luck in doing so?" That was one theory we hadn't considered, and one that had a lot of weight behind it. "It would stand to reason he or she wouldn't want to be caught with the ring, so they had no choice but to get rid of the evidence and possibly shift the blame to someone else."

You seem to be forgetting that your grandmother warned the Whitleys that someone would attempt to steal the ring from the cold dead finger of Caroline Abigail Whitley. My Rosemary would never have done such a thing if for one second she believed the sapphire couldn't do what the legend claims.

"Another excellent point, Leo."

I'm not used to all this praise, Raven. Are you still carrying that sapphire around in your pocket? Maybe the extra energy is messing with your state of mind.

"Nan wouldn't have risked outing herself as a witch," I said, glad that I had Leo to bounce ideas back and forth with. "She wanted that ring buried and hidden away from the world, which means we have to follow through with her wishes."

I'm sure you're going to argue with me on this one, but I have a very distinctive memory of the conversation your grandmother had with the old geezer.

Leo's issue with his short-term memory loss wasn't just short-term. With that said, I needed all the information I could get before consulting Rye and making some sort of decision regarding the ring.

"So, you *do* remember Nan warning Mr. Whitley about the ring."

Let's just say it's coming back to me in bits and pieces. I recall your grandmother receiving a call from Mr. Whitley, but I didn't pay much attention to the conversation. Honestly, there wasn't much to it at the time…and that leads me to believe the ring isn't as all powerful as good ol' Arthur thinks it is.

That came as quite a relief, but I still needed to be sure that magic wasn't about to be attempted by the hand of a human. After all, Nan wouldn't have given him the warning to begin with unless there was some truth to the sapphire's power.

How much more damage could a human do than you when it comes to…oops. Did I say that aloud? I think I've gone too long without smoking some of my premium organic catnip in my pipe.

"That's what I'm worried about, Leo—the damage a human can cause when trying his or her hand at a spell." I couldn't contain my huff of frustration, so I reached into my skirt pocket for my cell phone. Before I could place a call to my mother—

which, by the way, wasn't my first choice—a knock came at the door. It was still too early for Liam to show up for our date, so I made my way across the hardwood floor wondering who it might be. "We need some answers, and Mom might know some of the Whitley family history. I know how hard it is for me to keep my secret, so I can only imagine the struggle the Whitleys had in keeping such a secret under wraps from their friends. Maybe Mr. Whitley let it slip to someone that he had set up a security system in the crypt. Honestly, it could have been anyone who tried to steal the ring."

You're missing the point, Raven. No one stole it for their own personal gain. Whoever desecrated the Whitley crypt ended up tossing the ring away into a basket of cheap costume jewelry. They had a reason for doing so.

I slipped my phone back into my pocket before opening the door to find that Ted was standing on the doorstep, his perpetual frown firmly in place. I'd come to know that he didn't smile often—only when greeting friendly people on the street— so I no longer worried that the world was ending every time he frowned.

The world might very well be ending. You didn't hear a raccoon talk like a gangster. That has a way of putting things into perspective that you'll never understand.

"Hi, Ted. Were you able to talk with Ivan?"

"Yes."

I sighed and took a step back, allowing Ted to enter.

Smart. This might take a while. Talking to Ted is like pulling teeth. I, for one, am going to need something to numb the pain. Where's my Honduras stash?

"What did Ivan have to say, Ted?" I asked, closing the door behind him while anxiously waiting to hear his answer. I walked over to the overstuffed chair and took a seat, resting my elbows on my knees while wrapping my fingers around my coffee cup. The palm of my hand still tingled from my visit to the Whitleys, but I had a feeling that it had everything to do with discovering that the pricey ring harnessed energy of the earth. "Please tell me that Ivan saw who robbed the grave of Caroline Abigail Whitley."

"Caroline Abigail Whitley."

Ted remained standing, his long arms hanging straight down his side. I foolishly waited for him to continue explaining himself, but realized that he was waiting for another question.

"Yes, Caroline Abigail Whitley's burial chamber," I prodded Ted, scooting forward a bit more on my seat. "Who stole her remains and all of her jewelry?"

"Caroline Abigail Whitley."

Oy vey. Maybe dealing with a raccoon from Brooklyn wasn't so bad, after all.

"Ted, I know the Whitley family crypt was the target. I'm asking you who was responsible for robbing the grave."

Maybe we should head back to the garage sale tomorrow. It's the last day, you know. And if the sapphire ring was in a basket of costume jewelry, maybe Caroline Abigail Whitley's bones are in a pile of Halloween decorations. Get it? A pile of bones?

I shot Leo an exasperated look, but he had just made another very good point. I shuddered at the thought of someone taking real bones and mixing them with plastic props. Unfortunately, I had a sinking feeling that this situation was about to get worse. Ted's frown had deepened, and I'd come to accept that this time I should really worry about the world ending.

"Ted?"

"I don't know how much clearer I can be, Ms. Raven."

Time out! Don't let that oversized Crayola say one more word. I can see where this is going, and it's leading straight to the talking garbage eater.

"You weren't just repeating after me, were you, Ted?" I asked cautiously, gripping my coffee cup a bit tighter so that I could brace myself for his answer. "Caroline Abigail Whitley came back through the veil last night, didn't she?"

"Yes, Ms. Raven."

Oh, this wasn't good. At all. I could only assume that Caroline Abigail Whitley was attempting to utilize the sapphire's power to regain her earthly form. If that was the case, then where was she?

I know exactly where she is, Raven! Don't you see? This has turned into a rescue mission! Caroline Abigail Whitley is using that poor garbage eater as her way to reenter our realm of existence. We must save him!

Chapter Ten

"PLEASE TELL LEO that unless Caroline Abigail Whitley had some powerful Druid utilize a specific spell to reincarnate her at the exact moment she came through the veil, then her soul is definitely not inside of a talking raccoon," Rye said in exasperation, his deep voice coming over the line of my cell phone loud and clear. "Besides, the raccoon in question is—"

"Oh, shoot," I muttered, interrupting Rye as I made my way to the window. "Hold on just a sec."

The sound of a truck door closing told me that I'd let time slip by and that Liam had arrived for our date on time. Sure enough, he was already walking up the small path to the front door.

Leo had immediately taken a hit off his meerschaum pipe loaded with catnip the moment Ted had left the house, who was currently armed with a few more simple and straightforward questions for Ivan the Reaper. It would have been a lot easier if I'd been able to speak with Ivan myself, but Ted went on and on about the reaper's rules and regulations when it came to conversing with members of the mortal realm.

Trust me, it had been easier to send Ted than to argue the intricacies of the reality that I was also part of the supernatural realm.

"Rye, I've got to go. Liam just pulled up to the cottage for dinner. Please go back to the crypt and see if you can't locate the ghost or whatever Caroline Abigail Whitley has returned as. Heck, she might just have all the answers we need to set things right. I can't imagine she wants to remain here now that she understands what awaits her in the afterlife."

If you ask me, everything has already been set right. The ring obviously didn't work for whoever stole it, the moneybag geezer has the book secured inside his own version of Fort Knox disguised as a waterfront property, and the resident warlock seems pretty convinced Caroline Abigail Whitley didn't inhabit a helpless raccoon's body. Unfortunately, that means the garbage eater isn't quite so help-less...and now I've got to come up with a plan to waylay him. You realize he's actually patient zero, right? No one will ever know it was me who saved the world.

I disconnected the call before Rye could say anything else, having already explained my plan to Leo. He didn't necessarily agree, which was why he'd gotten into his Honduras stash and was currently stretched out on his back with his miniature legs sticking up in the air as if he'd fallen out of the sky that way.

"Leo, you're just upset because I'm about to tell Liam the truth."

I wasn't actually going to tell him the *truth* truth. I had just decided that it was best to give an accurate account of details regarding my visit with Mr. Whitley, though. The one factor that made all the difference here was that I had possession of the magical ring, and Liam didn't necessarily need to know that. It was just added reassurance that no human would be able to attempt any kind of ritual that would have them somehow releasing the energy harnessed inside of the sapphire with catastrophic results.

There are so many holes in your theory, I might have to start referring to this case as Swiss cheese of the brain. Did I mention how I hate the smell of aged Swiss cheese? If I wasn't so comfortable, I'd be hacking up a hairball right now just at the thought of taking a whiff of the rancid stuff.

"Leo, we need help from someone who knows all the residents," I pointed out, having realized that Rye, Heidi, and myself were limited on vital information due to the length of time we'd been in town. Leo wasn't helping, especially in his condition. As for Ted, I'd sent him out with a list of questions to ask Ivan regarding the restless spirit of Caroline Abigail Whitley. "Liam might not regularly patrol the waterfront properties on the other side of town, but he would definitely have heard some rumblings if such an old myth about the Whitley family seeking eternal youth had any truth to the tales."

You make things so darn complicated.

"Complicated would be if I used witchcraft on top of Rye's séance gone wrong and a possible flubbed spell cast on a hex bag," I countered in all seriousness. I'd truly thought that my losing streak had ended, but I wasn't going to try my hand at another spell until I was positive that the hex bag had no part in this predicament we'd found ourselves in. "Telling Liam everything from a purely holistic point of view can't hurt anything. Everyone knew that Nan was into holistic medicine, so adding on precious gems shouldn't be much of a stretch."

You might have a point about laying off the more complicated spells until you get a handle on the easier stuff...like conjuring me up a plate of freshly prepared tuna.

"I already gave you dinner," I said, walking over to the door before accepting that Leo had been trying to trick me into serving him two dinners. "Not nice, Leo."

Liam was going to think that Leo was hacking up a hairball,

when in reality he was just laughing. Strange laugh, but at least he wasn't carrying on about the talking raccoon anymore.

"Hey there, handsome," I greeted Liam with a smile. He immediately stepped up onto the large slab of stone that served as my welcoming mat for the cottage before wrapping his arms around my waist and pulling me close. "How was your day?"

"Better now that I'm here with you." Liam leaned down and claimed my lips, warmth spreading through my body that had nothing to do with the energy harnessed inside that old ring. He finally pulled away only to press his lips against my forehead before taking my hand. I pulled him inside the cottage behind me before I spun to close the door. "I ended up having to run over to Monty's place. Someone tried to break into his garage, but whoever it was didn't manage to get in."

Whatever you do—don't ask. We talked about opening up cans of worms, and I don't like those slimy creatures. Do the right thing, Raven.

"Really?" I asked, unable to let this slide. What if it was someone looking for the ring? Had the person who robbed the crypt stashed the ring away, only to come back for it later? That was highly unlikely given that they'd tried to search the wrong house. I was now confusing myself with all the possible subplots, and I wasn't sure if any of my theories held any weight. "Doesn't Monty live next door to Otis and Karen?"

There's not enough catnip in the world to keep me sane during these cases. Do you know how many times we've almost died? Now we're dealing with a family seeking eternal youth, a reaper who plays bad poker, and a mafia-controlled raccoon apocalypse.

I didn't walk farther than the living room couch, knowing that we were heading right back out to eat at the pub. We usually went to the diner or one of us cooked for the other, but the pub had recently added a few things to their bar menu that we thought we'd like to check out. I wasn't hungry in the least, but maybe that would change once I told Liam the truth about the crypt—which I intended to do before leaving the cottage.

Wake me when the conversation hits a wall.

"Yes, Monty lives next door to Otis and Karen. It's a good thing, too, because Karen heard something outside of her kitchen window. She knew Monty wasn't home, so she called me to check it out." Liam stopped short when he realized I wasn't ready to head out to the pub. "Someone did try to jimmy the garage side door, but whoever it was had left by the time I arrived. I let Monty know so that he could take extra precautions for a while and keep an eye peeled. Raven, why do I get the feeling we're not going out to eat anytime soon?"

I smiled before leading Liam around the couch so that we could get more comfortable. I had to be very careful with my words, especially since I was such a horrible liar. This time, though, I was telling the truth—sort of.

"Liam, I paid a visit to Arthur Whitley after leaving the cemetery this morning."

There.

I'd set the tone, and the rest of this conversation should be relatively easy to carry on.

Thus is the optimism of youth. You must get the energy from the coffee. Keeping up with you is rather exhausting.

"I'm listening," Liam said cautiously, slowly taking a seat on the couch diagonally from my position in the matching overstuffed chair. "I wish you'd have told me beforehand. I could have gone with you."

And this is why leaving the good ol' sheriff in the dark is a good thing. He asks too many questions, and here you are offering up our next case on a silver platter.

"I thought it only respectful that I explain to Mr. Whitley in person what happened at the cemetery this morning, especially after finding out that your Mr. Meyers doesn't really talk with that side of the family." I relaxed a bit when Liam nodded his understanding, although it was clear he didn't think anything of substance had occurred in the crypt. "Here's the thing— someone *did* desecrate Caroline Abigail Whitley's final resting place. As a matter of fact, I'm pretty sure that she's not inside that stone coffin."

Nothing like shoving the good ol' sheriff back into the fire. Is he still breathing?

Sure enough, Liam remained silent. He was taking in everything I was saying with a grain of salt. At least, I hoped that he was. Granted, he was blinking rather slowly.

Too late to back out now.

"Let me start from the beginning," I replied before drawing a large breath and letting everything spill out. "Heidi and I went into the crypt to look for Leo, found the lid of the stone coffin shifted from its original position, and then called you the following morning. I know you didn't find anything disturbed, but we didn't just imagine it. And now I have confirmation of what we thought we saw. You see, Mr. Whitley confirmed to me that he and his housekeeper were the ones who put things back in place before we arrived at the cemetery this morning."

Liam rubbed the back of his neck as he took in this new turn of events, but I didn't want him to ask me questions just yet. Leo must have decided that he was too far away to observe Liam's reaction, so he'd waddled over and jumped up on the coffee table for a front seat view.

I should have kept some of my Honduras stash for after this train wreck. This is like watching a B-rated movie right before it gets to the good part.

"I'll give you the highlights as I know them, okay? Mr. Whitley's family, dating back to Caroline Abigail, had a sapphire ring in her possession that was said to contain a special energy that had the capability of giving one eternal youth. I'm guessing here, but I don't think she ever figured out how to harness that energy—not that I think it could ever happen in the first place. I mean, that's ridiculous, right?"

Nice way to cover your tracks. Is that a hive on your chest?

"It appears that Rosalyn Whitley discovered an old book in the family library on the different healing properties of precious gems," I quickly said, not wanting Liam to interrupt my story before I got to lay everything out on the table. With that said, I did raise my hand to my chest to check and see if Leo was telling me the truth. Liam was bound to know I wasn't being one hundred percent truthful if I started breaking out in hives. "Inside this book, which Mr. Whitley has in his possession, is an enchantment of sorts. It supposedly explains how to harvest the energy of this particular sapphire, and that it needed to remain buried for three hundred and eighty years to gather enough power for this spell to work."

"Raven, I don't mean to—"

I leaned forward and rested my hand on Liam's knee, successfully getting him to pause in his interruption of what would no doubt be excuses as to why this all sounded so crazy. Technically, he'd be right. In the last seven months that I'd been practicing magic, I'd never come across something or someone believing in immortality.

One of these days, I'll have to tell you about the story of Ammeline Letty Romilda. Now that crazy myth will have you curling your toes, but I digress. Carry on. This is highly entertaining. The good ol' sheriff's reaction to this next part ought to be stellar.

"Mr. Whitley fully believes that it could happen, and that's what really matters here," I stressed, hoping that I could get Liam to see this situation through an elderly male's perspective. It was the only angle I had that could unify my two worlds right now, because I really needed the additional help in finding out who was after the precious gem. "Mr. Whitley personally rigged the crypt with a security camera, believing that someone would try to steal the ring…which someone did. He didn't want this belief in this myth to get out to the other residents, so he went to the cemetery before we got there this morning to put everything back the way it was so that no one would be the wiser. Unfortunately, the ring and Caroline Abigail's remains are still missing."

Liam didn't immediately reply this time around, but instead sat back on the couch with a long sigh. It wasn't a frustrated sigh, but it was a sigh nonetheless. It looked as if we were probably going to end up skipping dinner at the pub in favor of heading back to the graveyard. There was no doubt that Liam would want to look over the crypt now that he'd heard my story.

You've definitely broken out into hives. Unless it's poison ivy. I should keep my distance, just in case.

I didn't miss Leo wiggling his backside to scoot farther away from me, but his bulging left eye remained fixated on Liam.

"Let me get this straight," Liam finally said, surprisingly without any judgement. Then again, he'd never once caused me to feel insecure about anything. "Some myth about a sapphire ring giving an individual immortality was passed down through the Whitley family for several generations, and Arthur Whitley dubbed himself some sort of crypt keeper. Someone eventually stole said sapphire ring, along with the entire remains of

Caroline Abigail Whitley, and Arthur doesn't want anyone to know about the family secret."

I have to give the good ol' sheriff credit. He can sum up one of your crazy stories in two sentences. That takes talent, Raven.

"That's the gist of it, yes," I replied with an assertive nod. I, too, leaned back in the overstuffed chair. It was technically the first time I'd let my muscles relax since last night, and it felt darn good. You know what else felt terrific? Letting Liam in on this current mystery we'd found ourselves involved in. "I mean, except for the fact that Clifford Meyers doesn't know anything about the broken security camera that Mr. Whitley installed. Unless he did, in which case he might be the prime suspect. Oh, and the fact that Ms. Stella knows all about the book, the enchantment, and the magical ring. You should also know that Mr. Whitley thinks I might be the culprit who robbed the crypt."

"Let me guess. Your grandmother was the one who gave the Whitleys the book regarding holistic properties associated with precious gems, and he believes she told you about the chance of eternal youth."

He sure is quick on his feet, isn't he? I'm impressed. I wouldn't have known that by how he danced at the New Year's Eve bash the Bends family hosted for the local residents. You're lucky you have any toes left at all.

"Close, but no cigar," I replied with a grin. I mean, it was hard not to smile when Liam was taking all of this in stride. Even Leo would have to agree that this entire conversation had gone better than planned. "Mr. Whitley did call into the shop when Nan was still alive, and she warned him then that someone might try and obtain the sapphire ring sometime this year due to the old wives' tale about the length of time it took to complete the charging. Honestly, I'm not sure who gave the Whitleys the book or how long it's been in the family."

We need one of those white boards that the cops use on those crime television shows. How am I supposed to remember all these useless facts? Then there are the unanswered questions. Too much for my catnip-fried brain to grasp, Raven.

"You realize that in order to prove a crime has been committed that I'm going to have to take a look inside Caroline Abigail Whitley's stone coffin. That's going to require approval from a family member, and I'm guessing that Arthur doesn't want Clifford to know about what's taken place there." Liam didn't see too upset after hearing me out, but I wasn't so sure that creating an official crime report was the way to go. If that were the case, Mr. Whitley might actually try and convince Liam that I was the one whole stole the ring. "I'm also guessing that you didn't tell Arthur that you were going to let me in on this little secret of yours."

Not to point out the obvious, but the ring is still in your pocket.

"You know me so well that one would think we'd been dating for longer than five months," I said, a mixture of happiness and relief coursing through my body that Liam hadn't gone running for the door. "I'm not sure how to handle this situation, but Mr. Whitley definitely doesn't want this officially investigated, which was why he didn't report what happened to you. Hypothetically, a crime technically didn't occur if you can't look in the coffin to prove otherwise, right?"

Liam was a very intelligent man, and he also had very high standards when it came to his work ethic. It was one of the numerous traits I adored about him. That said, I really needed him to help the Whitleys—and yes, me—to find out who desecrated the family crypt without there being an official report.

Spit it out, Raven. You just don't want to get arrested.

That, too. With that being said, there technically hadn't been a crime committed if no one reported the vandalism and theft. Right?

Maybe you should mention the talking raccoon. That might have the good ol' sheriff thinking twice about filing a police report.

"Here's what we're going to do," Liam said, leaning forward and reaching for my hand. My heart began to beat fast against my chest at the decisive manner in which he spoke. What if he decided to open up a full-fledged criminal investigation? Mr. Whitley would definitely accuse me of taking the ring. Like Leo said, I even had it in my possession right this moment. "You're headed to the library, and I'm going to drive over to the crypt. Cliff does a good job of maintaining the interior, but I'll take a closer look at the stone coffin. We'll meet at the pub in around an hour."

What just happened here? Raven, I have to be hearing things. This particular moment in time is making me believe I made up that talking raccoon. No, that can't be. The masked bandit is real, he could teach Skippy a few ninja moves, and he definitely had a mobbed-up New York accent. Whatever this is…just make it stop.

"The library?" I was completely perplexed as to why Liam thought the library could help my cause. "Is there a secret room dedicated to the Whitley's lineage that I should know about?"

Liam flashed a wide smile my way and squeezed my hand in reassurance.

"As a matter of fact, there is."

Hold the frog legs with that meal! Did the good ol' sheriff just agree to join our merry band of amateur sleuthing or is my Honduras stash tainted with a hallucinogenic drug that will have him stripping his clothes off any minute?

Chapter Eleven

YOU KNOW, I'VE been here once before. It's very unnerving being trapped inside with all those rows of books and the deafening silence that's enforced by the sadistic overlord.

"It's a library, Leo. They call them librarians," I muttered, still sitting inside my car while parked in front of a surprisingly small public building that was positioned in close proximity to the local treasurer's office. As a matter of fact, Heidi's new office space was smack dab in between them. "There's only one vehicle parked out front. I guess I should have asked Liam the name of our local librarian. This tells me that I don't read enough. They could probably use some community support, as well."

I hate to call you on that one, but you do a lot of required reading. It's just not the kind that you enjoy. You have your reading assignments, and they all involve spells. Speaking of which, I'm sure you could have astroplaned into the library now that you're confident you didn't flub up the hex bag.

"Is that your way of insinuating that you still think I messed up the spell?"

I glanced in my rearview mirror to make sure no one was driving by so that I could open my car door and step out onto the street. The temperature was still a moderate seventy degrees, though it was bound to drop a couple of degrees once the sun set.

I had a one-sided conversation with a talking raccoon who thought he was a wise guy. You tell me.

I didn't bother to answer Leo as I palmed the keys to my car and began to walk across the road, bypassing the cobblestone crosswalk. The sooner I got this over with, the better. I kept expecting Mr. Whitley or Ms. Stella to pop up out of nowhere and demand that I empty my pockets.

The fact that Liam had so willingly put himself out there to help me find out who could have stolen the remains of Caroline Abigail Whitley, along with all the jewelry she'd been buried with, had come as quite a surprise and a welcome relief. I guess I could understand his inclination to help me, especially seeing as Mr. Whitley wasn't too anxious to file a report.

The moment Liam had driven away from the cottage, I'd sent a quick text to Heidi letting her know what was happening this evening. If all went well, I'd gather enough information that I might be able to pinpoint who else besides Mr. Whitley, Ms. Stella, and Clifford Meyers might have known about the ring's legend.

It's not a myth or a legend if it's true.

Was Leo saying that a mere human *could* perform such a ritual with complete success? Could a sapphire that had been buried underneath the ground for three hundred and eighty years actually harness enough energy to provide eternal youth? I found that really hard to believe. Weren't all sapphires buried in the ground before they were mined? Does that mean all sapphires are charged with energy?

I've been thinking…are we in the wrong business? You do realize that selling the specifics of such a spell could fetch us millions. No, make that billions. Maybe we could make enough to buy the entire country of Honduras and make it the catnip capitol of the world!

Raven, I never thought I'd say this in all my years…but you might be a genius!

"I'm now thinking that you should have accompanied Liam to the cemetery," I murmured, slowly closing the distance to the double glass doors of the library. I kept picturing an older woman at the counter with silver hair and matching eyeglasses, and then wondering why she wouldn't have stopped by the tea shop. Didn't all librarians drink hot tea? If Leo kept talking about selling the spell for eternal youth, I was going to need a lot more than a cup of tea or coffee to get me through this case. "I don't like knowing Ivan is at the graveyard all the time, just sitting around in wait of souls to collect. What if he gets bored, sees Liam walking across the graveyard, and then…"

You really need a harness for that imagination of yours.

I barely held back a shudder at the thought of myself actually meeting a reaper. Hopefully, I didn't come face to face with him anytime soon.

How is it that having you under my wing has produced spirits, ghouls, and reapers? My Rosemary lived in this town for a very long time, but she minded her own business and stuck to her so-called holistic herbal tea business. You should try doing that sometime. Oh, wait. You can't, because you're some type of magnet for supernatural train wrecks.

"Complain all you want, but you love me." I flashed a smile before opening the glass door on the right-hand side of the double entrance.

You should have come with a warning manual and the proper PPE (Personal Protective Equipment).

I didn't bother to reply as I entered the library, immediately noticing the cooler temperature inside the building. In my previous life—you know, the one where I had been an ordinary woman living a very mundane life in New York City—I had actually been a pretty avid reader, enjoying anything from romance novels to the latest thrillers in paperback.

Nowadays?

All I did was comb through the family grimoire and various books on the history and ecology of our supernatural ways, because how else was I supposed to learn all the enchantments and incantations? Some of the special ones could even save lives, preventing certain individuals from being personally introduced to Ivan's home game of stud poker. Wasn't it my civic duty as a witch to help others if I had the ability to do so?

I don't know if I need to get my hearing checked or if you are actually starting to believe your own malarkey.

I guess Leo was accompanying me inside the library and not going to the cemetery to watch over Liam. Once my gaze landed on the individual behind the desk, I believed Leo might have made the wiser choice.

What. Is. That?

"Um, excuse me?"

The reason for Leo's disbelief and my hesitancy was due to the individual standing behind the counter. Maybe because Ted had been created from the wax figure of Lurch from "The Addams Family". That might be why the show was lodged into the back of my mind, but I was pretty sure I was looking at Cousin Itt from that same show.

Could it be a juvenile Sasquatch?

Leo had a point, given that the individual had his or her back toward us, but the long brown hair went well past the counter. I couldn't tell where it ended.

Who knew Bigfoot was living in Paramour Bay?

"May I help you?"

Sweet angel of mercy, it's actually Darth Vader…with the hairy head of a yeti!

"Yes," I replied after clearing my throat a couple of times. I thought Leo had summed up the description rather well, but the man who had turned to address me looked like any other resident from the front. Sure, the man's hair was long and his voice was rather deep and raspy, but he had kind eyes that were rather comforting. "I was hoping to read through some materials on the founders of Paramour Bay. Liam said that the library had a special room dedicated to the subject."

Comforting? I'd break out the silver daggers, if I were you. You know, I saw a werewolf drinking a Pina Colada at Trader Vic's. His hair was amazingly perfect. Cousin Itt could very well be one with that amount of hair. Then again, he is cleanshaven. Does he have an electric razor somewhere behind the counter to keep up with the growth?

Werewolves?

I did my best not to take a step back from the counter now that I'd rested my hands on the hard surface. It wouldn't have been polite to have this man sense I was afraid he'd bare fangs or whatever it was that werewolves did right before they attacked their prey. So much for Leo's words of wisdom that werewolves, vampires, and such didn't exist.

I was being sarcastic at the time. You are a witch who has seen ghosts. You're telling me that you didn't blink an eyelash that a reaper was stationed out at the cemetery, yet you're surprised there are werewolves in the library? You really do have issues that I can't fix.

"How is Liam doing?" the friendly man said, adjusting his rimless glasses to get a better look at me. It was hard to guess his age, because he had that kind of face that people might predict anywhere from thirty to fifty. Seriously, it would have been kind of freaky if he hadn't had such kind eyes. "I've been meaning to stop by the station and drop off the latest Stephen King novel that he's been waiting for, but seeing as you're here…I might as well have you give it to him, Ms. Marigold."

Let me first say that everyone in town called Liam by his first name. He wasn't big on formality, because a lot of the residents considered each other family. The librarian in front of me was the perfect example of what I was referring to.

Now let me share my reaction to the fact that a perfect stranger recognized me for the second time today—I was weirded out.

Granted, the Marigold women all had long black hair, emerald green eyes, and rather shapely figures. We were somewhat easy to recognize as one another's relative, but it was still freaky to have two strangers speak to me with such familiarity.

Welcome to Paramour Bay.

"I can definitely take Liam the book he's been waiting for," I replied with a small smile, having already known of Liam's reading obsession with Stephen King. There had been nights that we had talked into the wee hours of the morning, covering topics from favorite hobbies to our favorite food. I sure hoped Ivan didn't come in between Liam and his next book. "I seem to be at a disadvantage, though. You know my name, but…"

If he says his name is Yeti or Cousin Itt…I'm out of here.

"Oh, silly me. I'm Harry," he said, reaching his long arm over the counter to shake my hand. His grip was firm and enthusiastic, but somehow his long hair didn't move. It was like it was its own shroud. "I'll have to thank Liam for sending you my way. We rarely get locals in here wanting to know all about the founders of our great town. Come with me, and I'll show you everything you need to know about the Whitleys. It's a shame, really, how most of the family has left the area with the exception of Arthur, Cliff, and Elsie. Of course, Arthur is the only one who retains the family name due to birthright. There is also a family tree painted on one of the back walls that you might find very interesting. It sure keeps tracks of all the familial branches."

His parents named him Harry. They didn't think that one through, did they?

I'd barely heard a word Harry had said after he'd mentioned Elsie's name. I mean, I personally knew an Elsie. The older woman was part of the infamous duo—Elsie and Wilma—who came into the tea shop once a week. They were best friends, well into their seventies, who had standing appointments at the salon every Monday. Never once had anyone ever mentioned that Elsie was a Whitley family member.

Don't look at me. I can see your eyebrow arching in accusation, but I for one didn't see this one coming. For once, my short-term memory is not to blame. You realize this is cause for celebration, right? I'm so glad I hit the reorder button on the Honduras batch of premium organic catnip before we left the house. You should really remember to close your browser when you're done using the computer. It might save you some money on your PayPal account.

"Elsie?" I asked Harry a bit skeptically as he came around the island and began to lead me toward the back of the library. "Elsie Cranston?"

I'd like to point out that I find it hard to believe an elderly woman would have stolen the remains of the dead, looted the jewelry off the bones of a skeleton, and then decided to toss a priceless sapphire ring into a basket of cheap costume jewelry. One, she doesn't have nearly the strength to move the lid off of a stone coffin.

Two, she'd have to be pretty greedy and morally bereft to pillage the skeleton of a dead relative. Three, no one in their right mind would toss away tens of thousands of dollars based on the notion of some family ghost story.

I agreed with Leo on points one and two, but three? If Elsie thought she was protecting humankind by getting rid of a sapphire that harvested energy for immortality, she wouldn't hesitate for a moment to throw it away. She just wasn't the materialistic type to care about expensive jewelry.

"Isn't Ms. Elsie just a dear?" Harry said, his Darth Vader voice somehow sounding sincere. As he walked in front of me, I realized that his hair was longer than mine. Leo's mention of werewolves had me staying a step back, just in case I needed to harvest enough energy in the palm of my hand to protect myself. "We can always count on her for a large donation every year."

The Yeti has a dark side, Raven. He's luring you in for your community pledge of support. Don't fall for it!

Before moving to Paramour Bay, I had been down on my luck and three months behind on my rent. Sure, the tea shop brought in modest revenue, but no one in their right mind would think I had any real amount of money.

"And here we are," Harry exclaimed excitedly, stepping to the side once we reached a separate room where there truly was a hand-painted tree on the back wall with names written in calligraphy on the branches. "Isn't this room just splendid? I'll leave you to your research, but I'll be up front should you need anything else."

Harry's large frame disappeared behind me, leaving me on my own in a vast pool of information regarding the Whitleys.

I know that look.

"What look?" I murmured after looking over my shoulder to

make sure that Harry really had gone back up front.

It's the look I've designated as Emergency Catnip is Warranted. *You're about to make another one of those decisions that could cost us our lives.*

How was paying a visit to Elsie going to cost us our lives? She might very well have details that could solve this entire case for us, and I wasn't going to let one more minute pass that could potentially put Liam in harm's way.

Look on the bright side. Liam could always play Ivan a hand of poker in exchange for his soul. He'd have a better than average chance of winning, considering his experience.

Needless to say, Leo's comment had me turning on my heel. With a quick wave to Harry and a promise to be back soon, I was out the front door before he could utter a word and ask about my sudden departure.

It's a wonder I don't have whiplash.

Chapter Twelve

"Liam's not picking up his phone." I practically gnawed my bottom lip with worry as I walked up the small sidewalk that would land me straight on Elsie's front doorstep. "Leo, go make sure he's okay."

Oh, I get it. The good ol' sheriff doesn't answer his phone, so now you're all worried Ivan has escorted his soul across the finish line. I engage in a one-sided conversation with a talking raccoon and you chalk it up to ingesting too much catnip. I see whose side you're on. I should let that flea-infested rabid masked bandit eat your little sheriff boy.

"This is serious, Leo. What if whoever desecrated the crypt went back to the scene of the crime? Liam might have been ambushed."

And that's a bad thing for me, how?

The colorful flowers planted along both sides of the sidewalk didn't brighten my mood any. The bumblebees were still hopping from one floral delight to another without a care in the world, regardless that early evening had set in and the sun would be setting in under thirty minutes. I found myself envious of the yellow and black winged insects, because all I could imagine right now was Liam's soul being ripped out of his body by a grim reaper.

Okay, that's just sad and a little bit morbid. It's got to be be-

cause you watched too many horror movies as a kid. Your mother did a terrible job of raising you. I can't take your whining anymore. I'll go to the graveyard to check on the good ol' sheriff. You owe me, though. If I see another talking raccoon, I'm going to run up a catnip bill you won't believe on your PayPal account.

This certainly wasn't how I thought my Saturday evening would be spent, but I was grateful when Leo took pity on me and agreed to check on Liam. After my conversation with Elsie, I might just head back to the cottage in search of a spell that could solve this entire case.

I'd given it some thought, and whatever spell I came across that could be useful would have to be one that didn't siphon any energy from the sapphire ring. It was entirely possible that the energy harvested inside the expensive gem was unstable. The last thing I needed was eternal youth while everyone else grew old and died around me.

Leo might have been right—my thoughts had become rather sullen lately.

I didn't waste time knocking on the door, going over in my mind what I needed to say so that it didn't sound as if I'd lost my marbles. Elsie might be getting up there in age, but she was still sharp as a tack.

"Raven, dear, what on earth are you doing here?" Elsie exclaimed in confusion, reaching for the handle on the screened door. She'd had the main door open to allow some of the night air to flow through the house, having told me time and again how she loved the smell of fresh flowers wafting through the house first thing in the morning and then again at sunset. "Wilma and I heard at the diner that you had dinner plans with Liam tonight. Oh, no. Should I call Wilma over? Did something happen between the two of you?"

"Elsie, you sure are something else," I replied with kindness, my heart practically bursting at the seams over the fact that Elsie would want to comfort me and have a bit of girl talk should the unthinkable happen with Liam. "We are just fine, but I did want to speak with you about something important. It concerns Arthur Whitley."

Elsie tsked her tongue on the roof of her dentures as she shuffled back a step, inviting me inside her home. There was the slightest scent of lavender mixed with the heavy odor of lemon Pledge emanating from every wooden surface in the entire house.

"What has that old fool gone and done now?"

"I'm not quite sure, and that's why I wanted to talk with you." I slowly followed Elsie past the living room and into a small kitchen that had been painted yellow many, many years ago. The bright color had long since faded from its once cheery tone, and I found myself being transported back in time to the 1960s. I was a sucker for nostalgia, too, so my fingers itched to spin the heavily-laden lazy Susan that was positioned in the middle of Elsie's round kitchen table. "I didn't even know that you were related to Mr. Whitley until I'd stopped in at the library."

"And how is my Harry? Isn't he the nicest young man? Don't get me wrong. I'd really like it if he cut that long hair of his, but I try to pick my battles. I'm not so old that I don't remember what it was like to be young and carefree."

Elsie didn't sit down at the table, but instead walked over to the stove to heat up some water. I didn't have the heart to tell her that I couldn't stay for a cup of tea that I'd sold her, so I had no choice but to resign myself for staying a good twenty to thirty minutes. Hopefully, Leo would be back with an update on Liam before then.

It took a moment for Elsie's last sentence to register, and it was a good thing that I was already sitting in the chair or else I might have landed with a plop. Elsie mentioned old and young in the same sentence. Was it possible that Mr. Whitley had been right all along in that a relative of the Whitleys had stolen the remains of Caroline Abigail Whitley, along with her jewelry? I was still confused as to how the ring ended up in a fifty-cent basket at the annual garage sale.

"So, what has Arthur done now?" Elsie asked in resignation, claiming the seat across from me while she waited for the kettle to whistle. "The last time I spoke with that man was at his wife's funeral. No, maybe it was the family reunion we had four years ago. Time just slips by nowadays. Anyway, I always wondered how Rosalyn put up with him for all those years."

I wasn't sure where to begin or how much to tell Elsie, because she was bound to tell someone…especially Wilma. The two women were the queens of gossip in this town, and they were also my source for all local news about the residents.

It went without saying that whatever I said here at this table would be fodder for the gossip mill before "The Late Show" came on television.

"I have to say I was pretty surprised when Harry mentioned you were a Whitley," I began, taking the easy path first. I'd made a decision to walk the more difficult trails after I tested the waters. "I don't believe you ever mentioned your family before."

"Harry likes to spin tales and continually lumps me in with the others, but our family tree has a lot of branches. I believe Arthur and I are third cousins." Elsie focused her wise gaze on me, tilting her head just so as if she could read my thoughts. "Is this about that silly legend regarding Caroline Abigail's sapphire ring? I might be old, my dear, but I've still got my faculties.

Wilma and I heard rumblings at bingo this evening that Clifford had been asked over to the cemetery by Liam to investigate a disturbance. My first thought was that Arthur had something to do with whatever was going on. He's always been a bit obsessive about that ring."

"Long story short, Leo chased a mouse into the Whitley family crypt," I said, managing to squash the words together so that Elsie didn't notice my anxiety over the white lie. "Heidi and I ran in after him, and we thought something looked somewhat off with one of the coffins. I called Liam this morning to check it out, who in turn called Mr. Meyers."

"And?" Elsie asked, curiosity now written across her weathered features. We both startled when the tea kettle began to whistle. She motioned with her hand that I should continue while she went about fixing us two cups of tea. "There's obviously more to the story or you wouldn't be here with me, my dear."

"Well, there was nothing disturbed." I stuck to as much of the truth as I could in keeping with Heidi's best advice, so I went with it. "I did feel bad about the entire situation, so I paid Mr. Whitley a visit at his waterfront property."

"I see where this is going." Elsie gave a lighthearted laugh, the kind she usually gave Wilma when they knew something no one else did. "Arthur thinks you tried to steal the oh-so-powerful sapphire ring. He always did have a very unhealthy obsession over that old wives' tale. As a matter of fact, Wilma and I were in the tea shop the day he called your grandmother to ask her for advice on holistic gemstones. Of course, he was researching the old family myth about Carolyn's ring."

"You were there?"

Oh, this was a new one on me. I hadn't known anyone else

was a witness to such a call, and Elsie's confirmation had me relaxing a tad bit over all the information I'd been able to gather today.

"Rosemary dealt with holistic herbs, so she didn't know much about gemstones and their properties. It's not unheard of, of course, but she couldn't give him the confirmation he sought now that three hundred and eighty years were upon us." Elsie had poured the hot water into two cups, using the Chamomile tea bags she'd bought at the shop earlier in the week. She set mine beside my cup on the saucer before going to the counter to retrieve the cream and sugar. It took a few moments before she'd rejoined me at the table and began to finish her story. "Your grandmother warned him that if someone thought such an ancient myth was true that there would always be a possibility someone might try to steal the ring from the crypt. Rosemary also warned him that dabbling in such stuff had a way of backfiring on whomever was foolish enough to experiment with such things. Oh, we all had a good laugh over that call."

Elsie gave another merry chuckle, though she had no idea that my grandmother's warning had been given in earnest.

"I do miss our Rosemary," Elsie said fondly, having already fixed her tea to her liking. She took a tiny sip before ever so carefully setting down her cup in the middle of the matching saucer. She then frowned and pointed a not so steady knotted finger my way. "If Arthur tried to accuse you of attempting to steal that sapphire, you tell me right now. I'll gladly give that man a piece of my mind. He's just an old codger who doesn't know what to do in his old age. Why, Stella comes over here around once a week just to get a break from his constant badgering."

"You know Ms. Stella? I don't think she appreciated me

stopping by earlier this morning." I took a sip of my tea, yearning for coffee instead. "I didn't even catch her last name."

"Jenkins. Stella Jenkins. She is Nora's older sister."

I had to wrack my brain to figure out where I'd heard the name Nora, but I finally recalled that she was the nice teller at the local bank. Beetle had taken over the deposits, as well as the tea shop's books. I hadn't given him complete control of the finances, but he'd redone Nan's system to better suit our needs come tax time. Everything was always properly marked, categorized, and balanced to the penny.

It made me wonder if Beetle might be of help in this case, given that he'd basically done the majority of the residents' tax returns. His brain was always a wealth of useful facts, plus priceless details that not everyone might be privy to.

"Stella comes across as a bit crotchety for an old lady, but don't let that frown of hers fool you." Elsie rested her elbows on the kitchen table and regarded me with affection. It was a nice change from the accusing glare of her third cousin. "If you're worried about Arthur, don't be. Everyone from back in Caroline Abigail's day is long gone, bless their souls. No one outside the family probably even remembers that old wives' tale, and I highly doubt anyone would risk getting caught robbing a grave to see if it worked when he or she would need that book that Arthur hides in plain sight."

Had the sapphire ring not been in my pocket and the remains of Caroline Abigail Whitley not been missing, I would have said this was nothing more than a cute family story passed down from generation to generation.

But I knew better.

Not that it made me feel any better about sitting here fudging the truth with Elsie sitting right across from me.

It helped to know that Elsie thought I was here because of Arthur Whitley and his accusation. This way, she wouldn't be overly concerned and begin asking questions that would have Arthur disliking me any more than he already did.

This visit hadn't been a total waste, after all. I didn't believe that Elsie had anything to do with the mystery at hand, and she'd given me insight on Stella. Mr. Whitley's housekeeper couldn't be all that bad if she stopped in to talk with Elsie once a week, because this cheeky older lady wasn't anyone's fool. Her view of Arthur proved that, but what about her opinion on Clifford Meyers?

Heidi, Leo, and I all agreed that Mr. Meyers had acted nervous at the graveyard this morning. He checked off a lot of the boxes when it came to suspicion—he had to be well-acquainted with the family legend, he'd taken it upon himself to be responsible for the family crypt, and he worked as a mortician.

I mean, think about it.

Clifford Meyers witnessed death on a regular basis. His job couldn't be pleasant, and I'm sure it had made him ponder his own sense of mortality more than once.

Why wouldn't Mr. Meyers try to discover if the old wives' tale held any truth?

"I feel better having come and talked to you, Elsie," I replied with a smile, enjoying the tea. It wasn't that I disliked the herbal beverage, but the rich flavor of coffee was more to my tastes. "I hope Mr. Meyers wasn't too upset about having to stop by the cemetery this morning. If you speak with him, please tell him I'm sorry for all the confusion."

"Clifford's mother and mine didn't exactly get along, so I only see Clifford occasionally around town," Elsie offered with a sad shake of her head. "It's a shame, really. Families fall apart over the most foolish things, mostly for perceived indifference. I'm sure you understand, given that your mother and grand-mother didn't speak for so many years."

I shifted uncomfortably in my seat, not wanting this conver-sation to touch on my family. We had too many secrets that couldn't be let out into the real world. Come to think of it, I'm sure that was exactly how Mr. Whitley felt about his family skeletons.

Speaking of skeletons, we have a problem. A major problem.

Leo had finally returned from checking in on Liam, but his breathless statement almost had me spilling what was left of my tea. Elsie gave me a puzzled glance, but I'm sure she thought the slight slip of the cup was due to the mention of Mom and Nan's relationship.

I completely understand. Just thinking about your mother can cause anyone to get the jitters. She's not the most pleasant one out of the family line, you know. Can you move this along? We have issues, and I'm referring to talking raccoon problems, if you get my drift.

"I do understand the difficulties of family dynamics," I em-phasized to Elsie, not wanting her to think that I'd lost my marbles. For a moment, I'd thought Leo had been referring to Liam being in trouble, but it seemed that Leo had another encounter with the cute masked bandit. "It's not always easy, is it? I appreciate you talking with me, Elsie. I'd best be going to join Liam for our dinner tonight."

Cute masked bandit? Are we talking about the same garbage eater, Raven? Oh, I get it. Elsie put an added ingredient in that cup of tea of yours, didn't she? I always knew good ol' Elsie was overdoing her opiates prescription. There are times that she seems far too serene.

"You tell that handsome man of yours that I said hello." Elsie waved my hand away when I offered to help her stand, showing me that she was still able to do for herself. "And let me know if that Arthur gives you any more trouble. I wouldn't mind hitting him over the head with that book of his. It might knock some sense into him."

"How *did* Mr. Whitley obtain that book? He mentioned that his wife found it in the family library, but I'd love to know where it was originally discovered and if there are more out there. You know how I love to dabble in holistic remedies," I said, hoping to figure out another piece of the puzzle. Besides, it had been Elsie who'd brought up the subject. "The ritual concerning the sapphire ring was very detailed, and the book almost seemed to be one of a kind."

Really? I tell you that we have a skeleton problem, and your first instinct is to rehash where the old geezer got the gemstone hocus-pocus book?

I couldn't very well address Leo as Elsie escorted me to the front door, but I was now really confused and worried that I'd misunderstood Leo's original statement. I'd thought he'd had another run-in with that silly raccoon.

I did, but that's beside the point. You're not keeping up with me, Raven, and that's a problem. We might need to get you some coffee, stat.

"I'm surprised Arthur let you touch that precious book of his," Elsie said with a chuckle, pushing open the screened door. Dusk had fallen, and there were now precious lightning bugs flying around instead of bumblebees. "I'm not sure where all those books in the family library came from. It's such a shame that no one treasures the older books and knickknacks, isn't it? Well, you have a nice dinner with your beau, and I'll see you Monday after my hair appointment."

After thanking Elsie once more for taking time out of her evening to speak with me, I quickly made my way to the car. I'd parked on the street, so it didn't take me long to settle behind the steering wheel.

"Leo, show yourself right this minute and explain yourself."

Leo immediately materialized in the passenger seat, leaving a few strands of fur to float around him as his bulging left eye narrowed in my direction.

You only have yourself to blame, missy. I explained we had skeletal problems, and you somehow gleaned from my direct exclamation that I was talking about the garbage eater. Your knack for taking the obvious and spinning it into something unrecognizable is astonishing.

"Leo," I warned, somehow managing to say his name between my clenched teeth. My concern for Liam had tripled, and the palm of my hand had begun to tingle in that uncomfortable piercing manner. "What skeletal problems are you referring to? And please be very specific."

Well, let's see. Liam ran into Rye. At the graveyard. Inside the crypt.

Oh, this wasn't good. It was hard to swallow around the constriction that had suddenly formed in my throat, which just so happened to be the source of all my lies that had gotten me into this mess.

Liam didn't know my familial connection with Rye, not that we were actually related by blood. As a matter of fact, I'd left Rye out of the equation altogether. How could I get Rye out of this mess without bringing in my Aunt Rowena and the entire coven by association?

Raven, Raven, Raven. Do you think that's everything? I haven't even gotten to the good stuff yet.

"I don't know if I can take anymore, Leo," I muttered, starting the engine and practically lurching my car into drive.

I did a U-turn right in the middle of the street, hoping to reach the graveyard before Liam carted Rye off to jail in cuffs. This was the problem when lie upon lie was spun together to weave a story. Eventually a person—me—became smothered by them. Ivan would probably be standing at the wrought iron gate to greet me for my misconduct.

Stop being so melodramatic.

Leo was finally indicating that the situation wasn't as bad as he let on, and the tightening in my chest eased a bit as I finally drew in some much-needed oxygen.

"Okay, I'll stop letting my imagination run wild." I stretched my fingers on the steering wheel as I brought the car to a stop at the intersection. I didn't even take time to admire the cobblestone as I usually did, but immediately made a left onto River Bay when the coast was clear. "What's the good stuff? Rye talked himself out of the situation, and now I don't need to worry? Although, please tell me that Rye didn't use some kind of magic on Liam."

The resident warlock didn't talk himself out of anything. As a matter of fact, he was actually caught red-handed by the good ol' sheriff.

"What?"

Oh, yeah. It sure was something to see. The one and only Rye Dolgiram was actually trying to put back the skeletal remains of Caroline Abigail Whitley. You should have seen the look on the good ol' sheriff's face when he realized what was going on.

"I thought you said I'd let my imagination run wild, Leo!" This couldn't be happening. How was I going to get us out of this situation without coming clean with Liam? The worst part was that I'd been duped by Rye, because it sure sounded as if he were the one responsible for this entire mess. "This is absolutely worse than the scenario that I'd conjured up in my mind."

I'll admit, none of this sounds any good, but you suddenly flying off into a full-fledged panic wasn't going to help an already dire situation. Is now a good time to mention that Ted showed up just before good ol' Barney Fife drew his pistolero?

Chapter Thirteen

*Y*OU SHOULD HAVE *seen what a hero that grey stick of wax turned out to be, Raven. He positioned himself directly in between our resident warlock and the good ol' sheriff. It was as if he were willing to sacrifice his life. Wait just a toad's ribbit. Does Ted even have a soul to lose? Now that's a question for Ivan, if I can ever get an invite to that super-secret poker game. You know, I'm actually proud of that Crayola.*

Leo had been rambling on and on ever since he'd spilled the beans about what had gone down at the cemetery. I'd driven past the police station directly across from the tea shop, and Liam's vehicle hadn't been parked out front. I could only assume that he was still out at the graveyard with Rye.

"I can't believe you didn't stay to find out if Rye was able to talk himself out of being arrested," I exclaimed with exasperation, my headlights finally casting their beams over Liam's black F-150 that was still parked directly in front of the wrought iron gates to the cemetery. I breathed a sigh of relief when I didn't spot anyone wearing a set of cuffs or someone sitting in the back of the truck. It meant that Liam, Rye, and Ted were still inside the crypt. "Come on. Let's go see if Ted was able to somehow diffuse the situation."

Come with me. Spy on the good ol' sheriff. Report back. Yada, yada, yada. I wish you'd make up your mind already. You've got more moods than Dr. Jekyll.

It didn't take me long to shut off my headlights, turn off the engine, and step out of the car. Leo did his disappearance and reappearance, vanishing from the passenger seat and materializing by my side walking toward the gate. He would no doubt make himself invisible by the time we closed in on the crypt, but I was grateful for his presence now.

Even though I'd been in the same place last night and nothing bad had happened, walking through a graveyard with nothing but moonlight to guide my way was rather unsettling, even for me being a witch.

"Hold on a second." I turned back toward the car, heading straight for the hatchback of the Corolla. I reached inside, trying to find what I was searching for in the moonlight. I remembered full well that Heidi had thrown the flashlight back there when we'd gotten in the car last night. Sure enough, it was right where it had landed with a thud. "Okay. Let's walk to the back of the graveyard—quickly. Now that I know for a fact that a reaper roams the grounds, this place gives me the heebie-jeebies."

The soft moonlight was shining down onto the old tombstones, but at least the patchy fog from last night had dissipated. The deafening silence didn't help lighten the ambiance, though, and I strained to hear but one cricket for any sign of life.

Really? You want some sign of life in a graveyard? Probably not your best hunting ground for that, my dear.

"Stop it," I reprimanded, tightening my grip on the metal end of the flashlight. I made sure to carry it in my left hand so that I had my right available to harness energy if we were attacked. Of course, such a thing would have virtually no effect on a ghoul. "You know what I mean. It's creepy out here, and I can't help but wonder if Caroline Abigail Whitley's spirit left the grounds of the cemetery or we're going to come across her merrily strolling through the tombstones."

I'm sure the resident warlock has the answer to that, considering he was the one who recovered her remains. I mean, what is his major malfunction anyway? Who in their right mind would purposefully open a portal to the afterlife? And why hadn't he been upfront about discovering her remains?

"I'm assuming that he wants the same answers regarding his ancestors as the council did all those years ago before Aunt Rowena sent him here," I conjectured, grateful that Leo was by my side to keep my imagination from running wild beyond the realm of reason. I kept expecting a hand to pop up from the ground and grab my ankle at any moment. "Can you imagine not knowing who your parents were or how you came into your magic? It must be hard for him to—"

How ya doin'?

I might have allowed a small squeak to escape my throat at the sudden appearance of a…talking raccoon. Leo certainly hadn't been the one to speak with that kind of accent.

Raven?

Now that time I'd heard Leo's concerned tone loud and clear, and I almost expected to feel his sharp claws dig into my leg through the material of my skirt.

Of course, by this time, both Leo and I had stopped dead in our tracks.

We were probably halfway through the graveyard to where the crypts were located in the back, but it wasn't like we could go over the masked critter. And who knew what the twitchy animal would do if we tried to walk around him. He was currently sitting back on his haunches, holding what looked to be a half-eaten green apple in his grubby little hands.

Are you seeing and hearing this, Raven?

The raccoon was switching his gaze back and forth between me and Leo, as if he were finding our responses quite entertaining. I wish I could say the same, but I was pretty confident I'd heard that specific New York accent Leo had mentioned, and I'd come to the conclusion that Leo hadn't hallucinated anything about this critter.

You can *hear him, can't you? See? I wasn't hallucinating, Raven! Isn't that great news? That garbage eater is definitely a front for a mafia smuggling operation, and you need to zap him right between those beady little eyes right this second! Now would be good! What are you waiting for?*

Whoa, hold up there, Frank. The raccoon tossed the half-eaten green apple to the side and sidled up closer to us after twitching his nose, instantly causing Leo and me to take a step back in unison. I'm pretty sure Leo did that flickering thing where he disappeared only to materialize again in under one point three seconds. *There's no need to be zapping anyone, buddy. You're hurtin' my feelings, run'n away like a scared bunny every time you see me. You'z start'n to give me a complex while I'm only try'n to help you.*

"Leo, I think Elsie *did* slip something bad into my tea," I whispered in horror, wondering if I shouldn't take Leo's advice and zap the raccoon bald right this minute. We'd discussed rabies a time or two when Leo got into altercations with Skippy, but this was unlike anything I'd ever encountered before. This was a dire situation which had me actually contemplating if Leo was right about the entire zombie apocalypse. "Wait a second. Who is Frank?"

Who is Frank? He's standing right next to you. Just look at 'em, doll. The raccoon shook his head in dismay. *I've never seen anything like it before in my life. He could literally belong to Frankenstein. I mean, Rye warned me, but who can take that guy seriously?*

Rye? Oh, this explained so much.

My dear Heidi is an actual genius. She's the one who called it—this garbage eating masked bandit here is actually a familiar. You realize that Skippy might have to be relegated to second place as my nemesis? I mean, who in Hades calls forth a familiar who sifts through garbage and has ties to organized crime syndicates? Our resident warlock is more messed up than I thought.

I've got no beef with you, Frank. I'm just here to facilitate an outcome, iffin' you'z know what I mean.

A quick glance around the graveyard revealed that no one was near, so I stepped a bit closer in order to keep my voice low. The last thing I needed was for Liam to stumble upon me talking to a raccoon. He'd really think I'd completely lost it, and then he'd call the men in the white jackets.

Come back here! Are you crazy? That thing could have rabies, for all we know!

"What's your name?" I began, keeping my tone a whisper. "And then please quickly catch us up to speed on what's going on inside the crypt."

Are you serious, Raven? You're asking this garbage eater for information? Where did I go wrong in your lessons?

"Leo, we both know that he is Rye's familiar," I explained, not really having the time to do so when the two men could come upon us at any time. I turned back to address the raccoon. "Now, what is your name?"

Joey Butter Fingers, at your service.

Raven, I respectfully submit my resignation.

"Hush," I admonished Leo, not wanting to alienate Joey

when it was clear he'd been trying to help Leo all along. "Let's hear him out."

Aren't you just a doll, Ms. Marigold? Don't you'z worry one bit. Rusty Rye has everything under control, although he does give this old ticker of mine a stutter, not fors nuthin'. Get this. He found the remains of that dead lady next to the cobblestone wall behind the crypt. What are the odds? Anyway, he was putting that rattling old skeleton back where it belonged when that do-gooder of a sheriff waltzed right into the crypt as if he owned the place.

It was really good to know that Rye had been upfront with me all along. Of course, Liam didn't know that, which was why it was so important I reach the crypt before the situation got out of hand.

Are you saying that you'll need my resignation in writing? I guess I can have Ted jot down a few lines for me. I'll just dip my paw in ink and slap it down on the paper. Signed, sealed, and delivered.

"Leo, you can't quit," I muttered, once more scanning our surroundings. It was still eerily quiet, almost as if the crickets and the birds didn't want to spend time with the dead. "It doesn't work that way. Anyway, this is good news. You didn't hallucinate, Rye was telling us the truth all along, and it's looking more and more like someone else is responsible for the grave robbing of the Whitley crypt."

One, I liked it better when this garbage eater was a hallucination. Two, I blame the resident warlock completely for bringing—I can't even bring myself to say that ridiculous name—this mobbed-up masked bandit to Paramour Bay, and what exactly makes you think the séance didn't have something to do with this entire mess? Ivan has already fessed up that Caroline Abigail Whitley is roaming this graveyard.

Leo certainly had a way of slightly altering every fact I stated, but I didn't have to worry about setting him straight. Joey Butter Fingers had my back. Although, all things considered, that probably wasn't the best idea.

That she most definitely was, Frank. But that old biddy just crossed over for a bit to see what happened to her bag of bones. I just had a chat with my poker buddy, Ivan the Reaper. She's been safely back in the afterlife since Friday night, with the promise that her ring will be returned to its rightful place. That's why you're here, right?

Did you hear that, Raven? This garbage eater plays cards with Ivan. He spoke with his good pal, Ivan. Tell me, nemesis…does the death dweller extend an invitation to his weekly poker game to just anyone or do you have to be a loser first?

Leo had completely made this situation personal, but we still had a mystery to solve. Someone had robbed the grave of Caroline Abigail Whitley, somehow lost the magical ring at a garage sale, and then tried to bring back her remains before anyone was the wiser. Whoever he or she was…the guilty individual had no idea that I was now in possession of the prized gem or that Rye had discovered the hidden remains of Caroline Abigail Whitley.

You know about our games, Frank? I'll make it worth your while if you'z wanna work the game. How's your dealing seconds? We'z could clean up. You and that local squirrel gang have some type of ongoing turf battle, right? Tell you what, Frank. I'll find out where that bushy-tailed rat is holed up in exchange for you'z helping me bustin' this game out. How's that sound? You can be Franky Green Eyes.

"Listen, the two of you obviously need to work out your issues, but now isn't the time." I couldn't believe that I was standing in the middle of a graveyard on a moonlit night playing referee between two half-baked familiars who just happened to be an overweight cat and a raccoon from Brooklyn. "I need to make sure that Liam doesn't suspect anything in regard to the supernatural realm."

Oh, that's already been taken care of, Ms. Marigold. You'z bodyguard did an amazin' job of coverin' for Rusty Rye.

It pains me to show even a minuscule hint of curiosity, but why do you call the resident warlock by that name?

Rusty Rye? Have you seen that warlock cast a spell? It's like asking the Hulk to tiptoe through a china shop. Ain't gonna happen. He's so rusty when it comes to castn' magic, he does his best to avoid it. It's why I'm not hangn' around much anymore. Don't need to be, and I got myself a steady girl in the city. Now, if you tell me that we'z could work that game, I can see to it that I make it back to town at least once a week while we'z bust those guys out. What da say, Frank?

Leo had still been contemplating an answer to the familiar who now topped his list of nemeses when I decided to leave them to their own devices. I had to reach Liam and reassure myself that all was the same as when we'd left the cottage.

Walking across the graveyard by myself had me in a very vulnerable pinch, so I could only imagine what I looked like quickly making my way to the back of the cemetery. My skirt was probably billowing behind me, and anyone driving past might suspect someone was chasing me. Either that or they might actually believe they saw a ghost running through the graveyard under the light of the full moon.

I hadn't realized I'd been holding my breath as I ran until my chest began to hurt, but by that time something had caught my attention. Sure enough, there was a light shining from within the Whitley family crypt.

It was a relief to know that Liam, Rye, and Ted were still inside. The fact that Liam hadn't immediately carted Rye off to jail told me that I would undoubtedly owe Ted a very, very big favor that I would happily repay, if possible.

"Whoa, there," Liam said with a chuckle, somehow stepping right in front of me to prevent my fall when I'd stepped into a divot. "What are you doing out here? I thought you were going to go to the library and then meet me at the pub for dinner."

I couldn't very well tell Liam that Leo had come to fetch me when things had gone south inside the crypt, so I feigned catching my breath. He didn't release me until I'd nodded that I was okay and not about to keel over from running a marathon across the graveyard.

"I was at the library, and I also met a nice man named Harry who showed me the room designated to honor the founders of Paramour Bay." I saw movement coming from inside the crypt, and sure enough Rye walked out with a flashlight. Ted was by his side. It seemed a good time to fill all of them in now that I'd confirmed Rye wasn't in handcuffs. Besides, it wasn't like I could let on that I knew Rye had tried to replace Caroline Abigail Whitley back into her burial chamber. "I left, though, when Harry told me that Elsie Cranston was a Whitley. Can you believe that one? I thought it best to talk to her immediately to see if she knew anything about who might be responsible for stealing Caroline Abigail's remains out of the crypt. Rye and Ted, what are the two of you doing here?"

It seemed the right thing to ask, given the circumstances.

"It's the most bizarre coincidence, but Rye said he saw someone trying to jump the cobblestone wall," Liam shared, shutting off his flashlight now that the moonlight was casting enough illumination that we didn't need the artificial beams. "Rye checked it out, and found the remains of an old skeleton."

"I should have immediately called Liam or Eileen, but I'd overheard at the diner that Liam called Cliff this morning about a possible break-in at the family crypt." Rye gave a sheepish shrug, pulling off the story with ease. A little too easily for my liking. "I couldn't stand knowing that someone had desecrated one of the founders' graves, so I thought I'd put back the remains of Mrs. Whitley and then call the station first thing tomorrow morning. I guess it wasn't the smartest move."

"You're a good man, Rye." Liam then gestured toward Ted with a fond smile. "I was ready to take Rye away in handcuffs when Ted saw all the commotion. If he hadn't been here visiting your grandmother's grave, he never would have witnessed what had taken place and been able to verify Rye's story."

I'm sure I blinked twice at the cover story of Ted visiting Nan's grave when he'd no doubt showed up to the graveyard to play poker with Ivan. Thankfully, Liam's attention had been on the two men.

"I'll touch base with Cliff tonight. I saw him out front of the funeral home changing the sign when I was driving by, so he's probably still there. A crime has definitely been committed, and I'm going to have to write up a report." Liam gave me what appeared to be an apologetic smile. "I'm sorry for having to postpone another dinner, Raven."

What Liam wasn't saying was that he was apologizing for having to make an official crime report and potentially leaking the Whitley family myth regarding the ring. He thought Rye and Ted didn't know about the sapphire ring, and that was fine by me. Liam could also be apologizing for cancelling our dinner plans once again, but either way this situation worked toward my advantage. It would give me an excuse to go speak with Mr.

Whitley.

If Liam saw Mr. Meyers at the funeral home, it was highly doubtful he was the one responsible for attempting to bring back Caroline Abigail Whitley's remains. I had been with Elsie, so that left only two people—Arthur Whitley or Stella Jenkins.

I'm gone for four minutes negotiating with that mafia don of a raccoon, and you solve the mystery? No, I don't believe it. Besides, the old geezer all but accused you of stealing the ring. He also wouldn't have tossed it into a basket of cheap costume jewelry. Oh, and you should know that the garbage eater and I came to an agreement. It was quite cathartic. He'd make a good therapist. And given that we're both familiars to inept magical casters, it's in our best interest to stick together. Skippy is safely in the number one spot on my nemesis list.

"Rye and Ted, will the two of you come by the station tomorrow to give a statement?" Liam asked, allowing time for both men to slowly nod in agreement. Ted was staring at me, almost as if he were asking for my permission, but he'd followed Rye's lead. "Great. I appreciate it. I'll go ahead and give Cliff a call. I'm sure he has something in the family records that might indicate what items of value had been buried with the remains of Caroline Abigail Whitley. We'll go from there if we find anything missing, and also do another search of the grounds come morning during the daylight hours. Who knows? Someone could have changed their mind about committing such a horrible act, and he or she tried to make amends."

Who's left on your suspect list?

Rye and Ted bid their goodbyes, with Rye heading toward the back entrance of the graveyard while Ted began to walk in the direction of my vehicle. Rye had no doubt heard Leo's statement regarding the pact he and Joey had come to, but we'd have to deal with that another day. Thinking back to our phone call this afternoon, Rye had tried to talk to me about the raccoon.

Anyway, we'd ruled out everyone on the list except for Arthur and Stella, but I couldn't understand why either one of them would believe I was the one who robbed the Whitley family crypt.

Which is why I don't think the old geezer or that old bat had anything to do with the grave robbing. I know this is out of left field, but do you think Ivan could have staged all of this in his quest to seek immortality? Granted, he's a reaper. But we should consider that the sapphire ring could bring life to a spirit. After all, it harnesses enough energy to provide eternal youth. That's quite some feat, wouldn't you say?

"Ted, I'll drive you home." I called out the offer, wanting to reach Arthur Whitley before he heard about the skeletal remains being returned from someone else. I highly doubt he'd been able to fix the video camera he'd had installed inside the crypt given all the activity here these past two days. "Liam, do you need anything from me?"

The good ol' sheriff needs nothing. I say we leave him here to take his chances with Ivan.

"That depends," Liam said, looking over my shoulder as he watched Ted wave his appreciation at my proposal to drive him home. "Did Elsie divulge anything about the Whitley family and who might have known about the sapphire ring? I honestly didn't know she was any relation to the Whitley family, either. I find that very odd."

Come to think of it, I don't recall anyone mentioning Elsie's relation to the Whitley family, either. Granted, I have some major memory issues, but your sheriff is relatively young and sharp when he wants to be. Hmmm. I wonder if he's been digging into my premium organic catnip when I wasn't looking.

"Harry seemed to think it was common knowledge. Anyway, she didn't have much to say other than she thinks Mr. Whitley is an old codger who doesn't know what to do in his old age."

We are talking about the same old geezer who spends his hours watching the security feed to a crypt in a graveyard, aren't we? I've heard about conspiracy theorists, but I've never met one of those nuts in person before.

Liam chuckled, though I didn't miss the quick glance he gave the crypt. He couldn't hide his concern over someone going as far as to desecrate a long-standing family burial chamber for some old legend about eternal youth. It was also going to be very hard to explain all of this to Mayor Sanders, who liked to be kept up-to-date on anything unusual happening in his town.

Now there's a man we can add to the suspect list. You said it yourself—the man knows every little nuance of this town.

Leo's suggestion did give me pause, but something was telling me the answer rested with Mr. Whitley. If I'm being truthful, my assumption had more to do with the warmth of my hand whenever I thought of Mr. Whitley than it did with anything else.

There was only one thing left to do.

Oh, trust me when I say there's never only one thing left to do.

"Liam, I think it's only right that I let Mr. Whitley know what happened here tonight," I said, quickly laying a hand on his arm so that he wouldn't have time to argue. "I realize that Mr. Meyers is the one who tends to the family crypt, but Mr. Whitley has a right to know that the remains of his great-great-great-great grandmother have been returned to their rightful place."

See? That's what I'm talking about. You always select the choice that puts our lives in danger. If you truly believe that Arthur was duping us all along, and that he is the guilty party and somehow accidentally lost the sapphire ring with it ending up in a fifty-cent basket of costume jewelry at the annual garage sale, then we'd be complete nut jobs to want to go back to his residence. See how easy it is to make sense like a normal person? You really should give it a try once in a while.

"I don't like the idea of you showing up on the man's door-step in the middle of the night all alone. He all but accused you of being the one who stole the sapphire ring and removing a skeleton from this graveyard." Liam had been shaking his head from the first word that had passed his lips, but he'd known me long enough that I wasn't going to change my mind. "Take Ted with you. I don't want you going out there alone, and I want you to call me immediately if he says or does anything that has you feeling threatened or scared. Agreed?"

Agree with the good ol' sheriff, and then tell him that the old geezer offered you a cookie. Strangers shouldn't offer other people cookies. If they do, it's probably because they've poisoned those delicious treats. Oh, wait just a reaper's scythe! You don't think the old geezer knew all along that you had the ring and was trying to kill you for it, do you? It's a good thing you didn't ingest that gingerbread cookie.

"Agreed," I replied softly, leaning up and placing a gentle kiss on his cheek. Leo's flair for the dramatic had somehow gone up a notch. I hadn't thought that was possible. "And you should know that it's only around seven-thirty on a Saturday night. Ted and I might stumble upon Mr. Whitley and Ms. Stella having a dance party out at their place. You never know."

The image of that old geezer and old bat with the resting b—

I might have let a bit of energy slip from my fingers in the direction of Leo, but it was nothing more than what one would receive from a staticy blanket. Liam had been looking down at his phone, allowing me to get away with the small indiscretion.

Not nice, Raven. You also hit my tail in the same place as last time. It can't sustain any more damage, you know. It could fall off. Anyway, that image of those two are just as bad as your mother and Beetle christening the back seat of his VW. There's not enough bleach in the world to wipe away that visual disaster.

"Please keep your phone on you," Liam requested, holding up his own in kind. "I'll call you the minute I'm finished up."

"Will do," I promised him with a small smile before turning and making sure I didn't step in that divot that almost had me falling to the ground earlier. "Good luck with Mr. Meyers."

Good luck with the oddball? Seriously? We're the ones going to need all the luck, Raven. We're about to go toe to toe with the evil doppelgängers of Hansel and Gretel, who have probably taken over the gingerbread house and want to stuff you in their oven. I'm not the size of a turkey, Raven. Possibly a small chicken, maybe, but not a turkey.

Chapter Fourteen

I THOUGHT WE were supposed to bring Ted along as a sacrificial lamb?

"We're not going to sacrifice Ted, Leo." I was unable to keep the exasperation from my voice. We'd once again found ourselves in the driveway of the prestigious waterfront home of Arthur Whitley. There was a good chance he was home by himself, given that Ms. Stella didn't live on the premises. Elsie had made it sound as if the woman lived in Heidi's neighborhood. "I assured Liam that I'd bring Ted along, but that was when I was supposed to give him a ride home. He must have walked to the cottage, because he was nowhere near the front of the cemetery when we walked to the car. It's almost eight o'clock, and I don't want to waste any more time digging up Ted. For all we know, Mr. Whitley goes to sleep by nine."

That candlestick is probably sitting at a card table with Ivan and who knows who else, raking in all the chips. Just so you know, my Friday night next week is booked. I'll be scouring the graveyard grounds for their hidden poker lair. It's got to be there somewhere. I can't let that grifter raccoon bust out that game before I get some action.

I let Leo ramble on about poker and the fact that he hadn't been given a personal invitation from Ivan as I continued to scan the house and the surrounding area. There wasn't one light on in

Mr. Whitley's windows to indicate that anyone was home, but I couldn't imagine Mr. Whitley being out on the town. He was probably at the back of the house, watching television or reading a book.

Or the old geezer is planning what he'd like to do with his immortality once he gets ahold of that sapphire ring you're still lugging around. Seriously, Raven. We should have left it at home in the safety of the coffee table.

"I feel better having it on my person," I whispered, trying to gather enough courage to open the car door. The palm of my hand had begun to tingle, and it wasn't due to the keys I'd tucked in my fist. At least the warmth hadn't reached a dangerous point. "Between the ring's energy and that of the earth, it would only take a millisecond for me to pull the current I'd need to protect us should we find ourselves under attack."

Then why is it taking you so long to get out of this pile of junk you love so much? Oh, that's right. Because somewhere in that rattled brain of yours is a random cell of common sense still screaming for its life. You must have gotten it from your grandmother, because you certainly didn't get it from your mother.

When Leo put things in perspective like that, it was very hard to argue with him.

"You're right, Leo," I exclaimed with a bit of relief, though I did feel the need to tack on my reason for such an agreement. "Not about the common sense part, but because there's nothing here for me to be afraid of. I can protect us using the energy available from the earth, with the added boost from the sapphire if I need it. I've got this covered. Let's go."

I was out of the car and tucking my keys in my free pocket before Leo was able to vanish from the front passenger seat.

It always makes me leery when you become overly confident. Do you recall the last time you were this assertive? Let me refresh your memory. It was last night. You were dressed all in black like some crazy grave robber. We discovered an empty crypt, an old myth written in an ancient book, and possibly an irrational old geezer who seeks eternal youth. Now do you understand why I need my premium organic catnip every night?

I didn't even bother to reply, seeing as I was glaring at Leo through the driver's side window and gesturing rather wildly that he needed to get out of the vehicle right this second. He understood exactly what I meant, and I didn't miss the slight roll of his left bulging eye at my impatience.

What if we were wrong? What if it wasn't Mr. Whitley who sought immortality? I wasn't saying that men didn't seek eternal youth, but women were more likely to desire something so unattainable.

What if Ms. Stella was the culprit we were looking for?

You're forgetting that the overly stern housekeeper with that facial expression I shall not name was with the old geezer the night they covered up the crime for whoever really did rob Caroline Abigail Whitley's grave. Wouldn't it be safer to assume that they're in it together? Ohhhh, that could be a plotline for a Detective Columbo movie of the week! A housekeeper falls in love with her employer, they long to live out their years of eternity as their younger selves, and then they go around town killing everyone who knows their secret! Raven, do you have a pen? We need to jot this stuff down. Hollywood would kill for new material like this. Sweet angel of mercy, everyone knows they haven't found anything original lately.

"We are not going into the movie business, Leo. I guess we should be thankful for the small things, though, given that I'm in possession of the ring," I countered, taking a step toward the front entrance of the house. I could sense Leo by my side as we walked up the driveway and then onto the small sidewalk. "No one can try and cast the spell for eternal youth without it, and Caroline Abigail Whitley's remains were put back where they belong. It was nice of Ivan to escort her back to the other side so quickly. Whoever the culprit was must have had a change of heart, which plays into our favor."

So, remind me why we're here again if the danger has passed?

"Because we need to ensure that the person or persons aren't going to try to do something like this again," I explained, really uncomfortable with the fact that such a family legacy existed. A story like that could cause an individual to act without thinking things all the way through. "Heidi found a spell that could make someone forget a specific detail. It only requires a bit of energy instead of a material component, so I should be able to cast it without the subject being any the wiser."

Interesting. I guess he, she, or they could have simply lost the ring. Maybe a helpful bystander saw the sapphire ring on the ground next to Karen Finley's table, and said passerby stuffed it into the basket thinking they were helping a neighbor tidy things up. It would make more sense if that was why someone had tried to break into Monty's garage, believing he was the one to find the sapphire ring amongst his sale items.

"That is a pretty darn good theory, Leo," I surmised, easily picturing that scenario happening in such a town as Paramour Bay. "What if whoever desecrated the crypt did so in broad daylight while the—"

It was a good thing that Leo had remained invisible from the time he'd gotten out of the car, because he no doubt would have done his disappearing act when the front door suddenly opened with a jolt. Seriously, my flat black shoes with the purple flowers left the ground by at least an inch.

"Ms. Marigold, it's nice to see you again," Harry greeted me with that deep voice of his.

We had it all wrong, Raven! Cousin Itt was the culprit all along! Run for your life!

I didn't do any such thing, but I did draw a bit of energy from the earth to protect us, if needed. You see, Harry was walking toward us, his long hair jostling and flowing behind him as if he didn't have a care in the world. Come to think of it, he did have an odd vibe about him.

Why would he be here? You don't think Cousin Itt just offed the old geezer, do you?

Of course, I'd been wondering what Harry was doing visiting Mr. Whitley at eight o'clock on a Saturday night. With that said, my first thought certainly hadn't gone to murder.

Why not? Isn't that always what happens? You stumble over a dead body, drag me into a murder mystery that comes close to ending my ninth and final life, and then Heidi comes in to save the day? Oh, wait. That was the dream I had last night. I do apologize. Carry on.

I'm not saying I hadn't considered Harry turning into something a bit hairier, now that Leo had implanted werewolves in my mind, but I didn't necessarily defer to out and out murder with some kind of weapon. For some reason, I was more concerned with the business hours of the library. Had Harry closed up shop after Leo and I had left to come and tell Mr. Whitley that I'd been reading up on his family history? I was trying to make sense of this entire situation and coming up empty.

If Mr. Whitley was truly innocent and not feigning innocence about the whole desecration thing, Harry's recent visit would definitely have Mr. Whitley believing I'd been the one to steal the ring and the remains of his great-great-great-great grandmother.

Unless Leo was spot on in his assumption that Mr. Whitley was lying dead on his living room floor. I needed to play it cool so that Harry didn't make any sudden moves.

"Hi, Harry," I replied with a shaky smile, curling my fingers into the palm of my hand so that I didn't accidentally discharge the energy that had coiled within.

Smart thinking. I don't believe my tail can take much more damage. You singed what little tuft of fur covered the tip.

"What a coincidence," I managed to say around the constriction of my throat. Harry had come closer, though he stopped around three feet away from me. What I really wanted to say to him was that we'd never met in the seven months I'd lived in Paramour Bay, yet we'd just so happened to run into each other twice in one evening. I figured mentioning such a thing would definitely give away my apprehension, so I chose a different route. "What are you doing here tonight?"

That's your different route? You basically just asked him if he murdered the old geezer. Smooth, Raven. Real smooth.

"It was the oddest thing," Harry said with his Darth Vader voice and a lopsided grin. "I received a phone call from Arthur right after you left the library earlier this evening. He wanted me to finish copying the pages of Caroline Abigail Whitley's diary."

I knew it! Cousin Itt read Caroline Abigail's deepest and darkest secrets regarding her precious ring, and now he wants the power all to himself! Zap him, Raven!

"I don't understand why Caroline Abigail Whitley's diary would be at the library," I said, refusing to zap anyone until my hand was forced. Besides, I really wanted answers to my questions. "Wouldn't the diary have been handed down to her children, and then so on throughout the generations?"

"No, no, no," Harry denied rather emphatically, his long hair swinging behind him. "Warren Lawrence Whitley's wishes were quite specific. You see, all of the family's original items are to be stored at the climate-controlled room in the library for safe keeping. This way, the family's legacy of being the founders of Paramour Bay would be well-documented and preserved."

Narcissistic much?

"I see," I replied, having come to the conclusion that Caroline Abigail Whitley must have written down something very important in her diary regarding the sapphire ring. I made a mental note to go back to the library tomorrow and comb through every page to see if there was any mention of the family myth and how it might have gotten started. "Well, I don't want to keep you. I'm just stopping by to run a business idea past Mr. Whitley."

I wasn't lying, per se. I did want to run something past Mr. Whitley, and magic was my business…so the two went hand in hand, right?

Again, your ability to rationalize is stunning.

This was going to be the big test. If Harry went on his merry way, then Mr. Whitley likely wasn't lying in a pool of blood in the middle of his living room. I instinctively held my breath, waiting for Harry to make a decision.

"You have a nice night, Ms. Marigold."

I was seriously waiting for him to welcome you into the darkness.

"Wouldn't you be able to read his thoughts if he were a werewolf?" I asked quietly after Harry was out of earshot. I'd turned to watch him take his leave, suddenly realizing that there wasn't another car in the driveway. "Where is he going?"

We've been over this, Raven. Jeez. You were right when you said you were behind on your reading. Anyway, I only hear the thoughts of witches and warlocks. Werewolves and vampires? No. Although, before that necromancy spell, I could smell a werewolf from a mile off. Now? Not so much. My sniffer isn't what it used to be. Hey, how about that? It looks as if Cousin Itt is neighbors with Mr. Whitley.

"I'm in the wrong business, then." Who knew librarians were paid so much that they could afford waterfront properties on parcels of land that had to be worth at least a half million dollars? "Do you think Harry really lives in that house?"

Maybe he is a werewolf, ate the owners, and moved into a new lair. Or do wolves have dens? So hard to keep track of these things nowadays.

Harry was still walking up the driveway of a house located directly across the street from Mr. Whitley. I couldn't contain my gasp of surprise when the front door opened and out ran two small girls, both with long hair that matched the same color as Harry's mane. They came running outside, their squeals of delight echoing throughout the starry night.

I've seen it all, Raven—two mini Cousin Itts. Who would have thought it?

I sure hadn't pictured Harry having a family, but the touching scene in front of us had the warmth of my palm shifting to my heart.

You're such a sap, Raven.

"It's sweet," I reprimanded Leo, not wanting him to distract from such a tender moment. "Maybe Harry is just good at pinching pennies. Or the house may be his inheritance."

Or he killed the family that lives there and their bodies are buried down in the basement.

"You're so morbid," I whispered in incredulity, watching the front door close behind Harry and his two daughters. "Come on. Let's go inform Mr. Whitley that his great-great-great-great grandmother's remains have been returned to their resting place. Maybe he has a clue about which branch of the family might have stolen the ring…only to then have lost it."

Or we could discover Harry killed the old geezer in werewolf style. You never know how this will play out, Raven. It might just surprise you.

Chapter Fifteen

I *THINK I might have preferred to find the old geezer dead.*

I couldn't fault Leo for having such a low opinion when Mr. Whitley had answered his front door with a frown and an accompanying accusation.

"Did you have to bring Liam Drake into the equation, Ms. Marigold? Is he helping you cover up the crime of stealing my great-great-great-great grandmother's sapphire ring and her remains? He is, isn't he? You realize that when word gets out that immortality can be acquired through that precious piece of jewelry, people will come crawling out of the woodwork like the cockroaches they are!"

And here you thought I was morbid and had a flair for the dramatic. This goes to prove it can always get worse.

"Mr. Whitley, for the tenth time…I was not the one who robbed your family's crypt." We'd been standing in the beautiful kitchen overlooking the moonlit waves of water, not in the least bit relaxed from the calming sight before us. This visit probably hadn't been one of my better ideas, especially now that Mr. Whitley was all riled up. There was no way that he was the one responsible for the desecration. "Liam is informing Mr. Meyers as we speak that the remains of Caroline Abigail have been returned to her final resting place. I just thought you should hear it from me that there will no doubt be a criminal report filed on the sapphire ring after Mr. Meyers finds that it wasn't returned with the skeletal remains."

If I didn't know any better, I'd say that woman knows I'm sitting on the kitchen table.

I spared a glance toward Ms. Stella, who was tidying up the kitchen after Mr. Whitley had enjoyed a late meal. Sure enough, she was looking our way, though I don't think she knew about Leo being in attendance. She actually seemed to be staring at me with…frustration? Anger? I wasn't sure, but I did know that I'd overstayed my welcome.

"This is all your fault," Mr. Whitley accused me with a knotted finger, clutching the old leather-bound book he'd shown me this morning to his chest.

For a brief moment, I thought he was going to keel over. He'd gotten himself worked up to the point that a few veins had popped out on his forehead and caused me to wonder if he was going to have a heart attack or a stroke.

That would certainly be your luck, wouldn't it?

"Arthur, sit down before you wind yourself up into a tizzy," Ms. Stella scolded him from across the kitchen. It was the first time I'd ever seen her take the initiative. Then again, I'd only just met her today. "I'll make the two of you some tea while you sit down and hash this out."

She must have been a teacher in her former years. No wonder her facial features froze in such a position. I completely understand now. It's the same way I feel when I'm trying to teach you a spell for two and a half hours without any forward momentum.

Mr. Whitley sank down in a chair with a huff at the beautifully ornate table that could easily sit ten people, all but slamming the leather-bound book down on the hard surface. Within arm's reach was a folder that I had no doubt contained the copy of Caroline Abigail's diary that Harry had dropped off this evening.

The discreet cough coming from across the room told me I was expected to take a seat at the table, as directed.

I wouldn't say no, Raven. That woman has the pointed lip down to a science. I wonder if that's what she taught in school.

Truthfully, I was pretty sure I'd overstayed my welcome.

"As I mentioned earlier, I only came to share with you that the remains of your great-great-great-great grandmother were returned to her final resting place. I'm sure that gives you some sense of closure. I would like to reiterate one more time that I had nothing to do with the desecration of your family crypt, Mr. Whitley. I do appreciate you taking time out to hear what I had to say, so I'll just be on my—"

"Sit."

I'd been speaking directly to Mr. Whitley, so I hadn't been paying one ounce of attention to Ms. Stella. Her sharp directive had been said inches from ear, and I found myself plopped in a chair on the opposite end of the table from Mr. Whitley before I could even blink.

Yep. She was definitely a teacher, and she has completely earned my respect. I should take some pointers.

"I'll bring out some cookies while the water is boiling," Ms. Stella shared with a sharp nod before silently walking across the immaculate tile of the kitchen.

"You're the only one who knew about the sapphire ring," Mr. Whitley said accusingly, tapping his fingers on the leather-bound book in irritation.

"You assume that, but I did not know about the sapphire ring or its potential to offer eternal youth. Let me ask you a question, Mr. Whitley. Why would I have come here this morning to tell you about the desecration of the crypt if I was the one responsible?"

Mr. Whitley arched a bushy eyebrow as he carefully mulled over my inquiry, moving his hand out of the way when Ms. Stella returned with a small plate of gingerbread cookies. She made her way to my side of the table, setting down a small portion of cookies for me, as well.

"Eat."

My hand automatically reached for one of the cookies, pleasantly surprised to find that they were still warm. If I hadn't known any better, I would have said it was magic.

No magic. If she'd been a witch, she would definitely have fixed that expression of hers by now. It must be terrible to go through life having people assume you hate them. Unless she does hate you. In that case, I don't know what to tell you. Hey, what's that?

Ms. Stella began to walk back toward the stove where she was heating up the tea kettle, but I hadn't noticed anything strange. I then glanced toward the opposite end of the table, but Mr. Whitley continued to glare at me as if I were the cause of all his troubles.

The plate, Raven. Look at the plate, but don't be too obvious. That Ms. Stella is something else, isn't she? She's earned my respect, so therefore I will call her Ms. Stella.

"You could have come to my home in order to distract me from your goal—retrieving the book that holds the spell to eternal youth," Mr. Whitley exclaimed after having already eaten one of his cookies. "I don't believe for a moment that Clifford would have the audacity to cross me, and Elsie is too old to have moved the lid off of that stone coffin. My children are scattered around the United States, and they aren't scheduled to visit me until the holidays. So, young lady, that leaves you as the only suspect."

There was no helping me when the cookie I'd taken a bite of got lodged in my throat at the sight of a handwritten note on the cocktail napkin that had been carefully placed underneath the delicious treats.

Now probably isn't the time to point this out, but I don't know the Heimlich Maneuver.

Mr. Whitley glared at me over the table as if I were an imposition, but I was finally able to clear my throat by coughing uncontrollably. On the bright side, Ms. Stella once again appeared out of nowhere with a glass of water.

Isn't she nice? I was really wrong about her from the onset, wasn't I?

"The tea will be ready shortly," Ms. Stella reported to us before wiping her hand on her apron and turning to finish her nightly duties.

It took another minute for me to control my cough, but it was enough time for me to figure out what to do about the secret note and how to address Mr. Whitley's suspicions. I'd also sucked down at least half the water in the glass before setting it back down on the table, ensuring that it was in front of the small plate so that Mr. Whitley didn't inadvertently find such evidence of guilt.

Who knew that Ms. Stella could be so cunning? If she wasn't so old, Heidi might have had some competition.

You see, Ms. Stella had all but written her confession on a cocktail napkin. All was not what it seemed, though.

Is it ever? And I'd like to point out that we've never gotten a written confession out of anyone before. It's very satisfying, isn't it?

Before I could begin my explanation of how the culprit couldn't have been me, the doorbell rang. Mr. Whitley frowned before glancing over to Ms. Stella, who continued to calmly go about setting tea items on the delicate serving tray.

Do you think she'd wait on me hand and foot, bringing me catnip when I rang my bell? I have one, you know, for when we win the lottery and buy Honduras.

"I'll get it, Stella," Mr. Whitley said gruffly, using the arms of the chair to help him stand. He shot me another glare as he grabbed his cane. "You stay right there, young lady. We're not through yet."

I'll look the other way if you'd like to zap him. On second thought, I'd rather watch the old geezer get his due.

I feigned picking up my glass of water so that my out-stretched arm would cover the cocktail napkin, mindful of Mr. Whitley making his way past me and through the swinging door that I'd only ever seen in movies. Once he was completely gone, I quickly took the napkin from underneath the remaining two cookies and stuffed it into my pocket next to the sapphire ring.

Great. The evidence and the confession all in your pocket. You better hope the good ol' sheriff doesn't get frisky or else he'll be hauling you off to jail.

"Ms. Stella," I whispered harshly, making my way over to the stove where Ms. Stella was pouring the boiling water into a delicate china pot trimmed in gold. She didn't even appear nervous that she all but confessed, but rather confident that I'd keep her secret. "Why would you take the remains of Caroline Abigail Whitley, along with the sapphire ring, from her final resting place? What were you thinking?"

Ms. Stella might have earned my respect, but have you looked at that stern expression? I mean, who would think lips could be so straight? Let's face it…eternal youth would be very alluring, given the circumstances. Everyone has a weakness, Raven. Be gentle.

"I was thinking what any wise woman would in my situation," Ms. Stella responded without so much as spilling a drop of the boiling water. She then set the tea kettle back on the stove before reaching for the creamer that she would no doubt pour into the matching creamer bowl. "Arthur may never have the power of immortality. Whether or not it's an old wives' tale, I couldn't take the chance that he could succeed in such a manner. I took matters into my own hands by paying Harry a very nice sum to help me make the crypt look like a crime scene. Of course, that was after he had disassembled the security camera. His skills are so eclectic, aren't they?"

If Cousin Itt is anything like his father—Darth Vader—then he is not to be trifled with. You should tell Ms. Stella that so she knows to continually look over her shoulder.

I glanced at the doorway, knowing that I was running out of time. My first instinct upon reading the note had been to protect Ms. Stella, but she didn't appear as if she were in the need of my help.

We know who to ask to join our army against the squirrel apocalypse. Oh, did I mention that Joey is on board as one of our enforcers? He'll come whenever called. Unfortunately, that means we'll have to include the resident warlock into our plans, but we can always use him as a shield if it comes to that.

"Ms. Stella, I found the sapphire ring where you left it."

There.

I'd said it.

Annnndddd, why would you do that? Inquiring minds want to know.

"Well, at least it's in good hands." Ms. Stella continued to shuffle the items on the tray just so before she picked it up off the counter to take over to the table as if we weren't discussing the fact that she had been the thief all along. "Your grandmother was a wonderful woman, often selling me special tea blends for Mr. Whitley. I've come to hear from my dear friend, Elsie, that you've carried on in your grandmother's love of holistic remedies. I shall stop by your shop later this week to begin placing my orders. In the meantime, I'm sure you'll dispose of the ring in the proper manner."

Oh, yeah. Did I forget to mention that Ms. Stella used to be a regular visitor to the tea shop? My bad.

"You see, I slid the sapphire ring in the first costume jewelry basket I came across. I only temporarily removed the remains of Caroline Abigail to give Arthur something else to focus on. It was a drastic move that I debated on for quite a while, but it had to be done. I would do it again, if need be," Ms. Stella explained, having carried the tea tray over to the table. She began to fix Mr. Whitley's tea for him, which had me wondering why he hadn't made his way back to the kitchen yet. "To make a long story short, I had Harry return the remains to the cemetery earlier today, but he thought someone was following him. He hid them next to the cobblestone wall with every intention of returning after midnight tonight to finish the job. I will have to notify him that his services will no longer be required. I'm very thankful to hear that Mrs. Caroline Abigail Whitley has been put back into her final resting place."

I win! Did I call that or what? I guessed that someone purposefully stuffed the ring in with that cheap costume jewelry basket. I'm getting so good at this amateur sleuth stuff.

"You did all this because you didn't want Arthur to obtain this so-called immortality?"

"I've worked for the Whitley family for many years, home-schooling their children, and seeing to their every need." Ms.

Stella had finally finished her preparations and turned to face me, her expression as stern as ever. "Mr. Whitley is not the person who should be the first to achieve immortality, if it is in fact possible. No one should, for that matter. I did what I had to do, as I'm sure you'll do the same. Now, we must never speak of this again."

I was right again! Ms. Stella did teach children, and I bet they have the scars on their knuckles from her ruler to prove it. You know what this means, right? I'm spot on about this squirrel apocalypse, and we must take the appropriate measures!

"You realize that Mr. Whitley will never stop looking for the family heirloom, right? I mean, this affects me personally seeing as he truly believes I took the ring from his family's crypt. He'll brand me a thief in public, at some point."

Stop making this about you, Raven. Now that Joey has been confirmed as a non-threat, we need to concentrate on Skippy and his ninja warriors. It's good to know that Cousin Itt can be bribed with money. I might need to raid your bank account at some point.

Leo could have rambled on and on about the squirrel apocalypse, but it wouldn't have stopped the various scenarios of the aftermath of this predicament floating through my mind. I mean, the accusations would follow me throughout the rest of my life. I was very lucky I wasn't the hyperventilating type. It was enough to make anyone panic.

Really? He's an old geezer who's spouting on and on about immortality spells. Trust me, the spotlight won't be on you. I've got to hand it to Ms. Stella. She sure is one smart cookie. Get it? Did you see the double entendre there? Really, it could be a triple if you note that she is the cook here.

"I've taken care of that, as well." Ms. Stella lowered her head and gave me that stern look that I remembered well from all of my schoolteachers. "The rest is up to you. Silence is golden, Ms. Marigold."

That was a special warning of some kind, wasn't it? Ms. Stella kind of reminds me of Ted, only answering with what she wants and leaving us guessing the other ninety percent of the time.

We could all hear Mr. Whitley calling Ms. Stella's name as he got closer and closer to the swinging door of the kitchen. I had enough time to make it back to my chair, while Ms. Stella took her time removing her apron. Her purposeful actions made it seem as if the last three minutes hadn't occurred.

Watching an expert in action is very thrilling, isn't it?

"Stella," Arthur exclaimed, frustration lacing his tone as he shuffled through the door. He didn't even give me a first glance, let alone a second. He had zeroed in on his housekeeper while holding up some type of photograph. "This was left on the front step. It's proof there was no ring buried with my great-great-great-great grandmother. How could this be? It was documented throughout generations and generations. I just don't understand."

This is Ms. Stella's doing. I can smell her satisfaction from here.

"I'm so sorry to hear that, Arthur," Stella said with what sounded like complete sincerity. She'd folded her apron and slid it into one of the numerous drawers underneath the counter. "What proof was given? I'm sure we can have Harry double check the records over at the library."

The old geezer is playing right into her hands.

"No need," Arthur denied as he reclaimed his chair with a huff. "I'm pretty sure that imbecile Clifford left this here to rub it in my face. This here is a picture of one of our cousins named Margaret from when she was younger. Look here. Right there on her finger is the sapphire ring. All these years, the other side of the family had the ring in their possession and no one had been the wiser."

"Do you believe that Clifford thinks you were the one to rob the family crypt?" Stella asked without any indication she knew any different. She even came over to the table and gently rested a hand on his shoulder. "Here. Let me warm up your tea for you."

Did you just sense the shift in the ambiance? I'm suddenly catching a whiff of something.

If I hadn't witnessed the small bit of affection myself, I never would have put two and two together. It wasn't that Ms. Stella believed Mr. Whitley was a bad man. It had never been about that at all. Ms. Stella's crimes had all been done in the name of love.

Hairball.

It thought it was rather sweet. Ms. Stella had become fond of her employer, and I'm sure the two had grown close over the years after the death of his wife so many years ago. It dawned on me that Ms. Stella didn't go to Elsie's house to vent about Mr. Whitley, but most likely to keep up the thin veneer of a charade casting them as simply employee and employer.

"Thank you, Stella." Arthur frowned as he set the old picture down next to the leather-bound book. He rested his hand on the old tome that had stood the test of time in what was now easily recognizable as regret. "The fleeting chance of eternal youth is gone. Young lady, it looks as if I owe you an apology. The sapphire ring had never been buried with my great-great-great-great grandmother. Three hundred and eighty years of investment wasted. What a shame."

I munched on a cookie while figuring out which direction to take this conversation, because even I could still spot the loose ends.

You could always ignore them. That usually works for me. It did with the garbage eater. I didn't make a big deal of what you thought was a hallucination. I didn't panic. Not in the least. I let the day run its course, and in the end that masked bandit turned out to be an ally.

I so wanted to argue with Leo's version of events, but now wasn't the time.

"Arthur, I realize that my grandmother was into holistic remedies and the benefits that can come from certain gemstones, but I'm not so sure eternal youth is one of them. I honestly don't believe immortality exits." I set down my half-eaten cookie to try and articulate one of the loose threads. It wouldn't do to have Mr. Whitley pull on one and unravel this entire cover-up. "Will you speak with Mr. Meyers about the picture? How sure are you that he was the one to leave the photograph on your front step?"

I realize that you can't see the photo from where you're sitting, but trust me…that mortician definitely takes after his father's side of the family.

"Oh, it was that imbecile, alright," Mr. Whitley grumbled while Ms. Stella walked back to the table with a clean teacup in hand. "But I'm not going to give him the satisfaction of asking him about the ring. That's what he wants—to see me squirm. I'd be walking into his trap if I brought up the topic, and that won't happen…ever."

I hadn't been too sure that Ms. Stella could even smile, but there did seem to be a lift to the corner of her thin lip. She'd known all along how to play this situation so that Mr. Whitley wouldn't continue his quest to find the ring. In his mind, the sapphire was useless now that it hadn't been buried under ground for three hundred and eighty years. Of course, family dynamics played a big part in Mr. Whitley's decision to let bygones be bygones, but Ms. Stella had known that all along.

"I'm sure we'll find something to do for our remaining years, Arthur." Ms. Stella had finished preparing his hot tea before purposefully tying up the remaining loose end to give both of us peace of mind going forward. "I suppose whoever attempted to rob the grave got the surprise of his life to find that the sapphire ring wasn't inside. Who do you suppose it was, Arthur?"

Mistress of Manipulation. That's what I'm going to dub her. I so need to take notes.

It wasn't that Ms. Stella was manipulating, but rather leading Mr. Whitley down the right path in his old age. She'd known all along that had the ring and spell worked, she would have been left alone in her old age only to lose the love of her life to eternal youth. Immortality wasn't all it was cracked up to be, though.

Selfish or giving?

I guess the answer was subjective, but I still played a part in this mystery. I now had a sapphire ring in my possession that could potentially offer someone immortality. I guess it was time I learn a binding spell.

I feel another hairball coming up.

"If Clifford has known all along that the ring wasn't inside the stone coffin, and it wasn't this young lady…then my bet is on Elsie's side of the family. She is getting up there in years," Mr. Whitley pointed out, taking a sip of the tea that Ms. Stella had just made for him. "I'm sure she could have gotten one of her nephews to come to town to do her dirty work, but we have that family reunion coming up next year. It wouldn't do for me to start slinging accusations around and dividing the family members into factions."

Getting back to this binding spell, I'm not going to be happy if I find I can't speak afterward. You're liable to bind my voice box. I appreciate you giving my tail a rest, but that seems a bit extreme, don't you think?

"No, it wouldn't do to be the cause of more family drama, Arthur." Stella gestured toward the book, wiggling her fingers until Mr. Whitley begrudgingly handed it over to her. "I'll go put this back where it belongs while the two of you finish up here. It's getting late, and you need your sleep. I'll be back at seven o'clock sharp tomorrow morning so that we can watch the sailboat race from the patio. I'll make us some fresh blueberry muffins."

Isn't the Mistress of Manipulation just as happy as a clam?

That she was, and rightly so. Ms. Stella had averted a disaster in the making, she had been able to keep the love of her life by her side for their remaining years on earth, and she'd done so without leaving one dangling thread. Her determination and attention to detail was to be admired.

I'm pretty sure there's one thread left, but the Mistress of Manipulation seems to be leaving the good ol' sheriff up to you.

Oh, shoot. Leo was talking about the crime report that Mr. Meyers—who still correctly believed the ring had been buried in the stone coffin with Caroline Abigail Whitley—would no doubt file with Liam regarding the missing ring.

"Mr. Whitley, I should be going," I announced before quickly standing from the chair. "I am sorry that things didn't work out quite as you intended."

"That's life, dear," Arthur replied as he continued to enjoy his tea. "It's a lesson everyone should take to heart."

"There's also always a silver lining," Ms. Stella pointed out with a glimmer in her eye, still standing at the swinging door waiting to escort me from the house. "Sometimes silver can be worth more than sapphires."

Look at that. The Mistress of Manipulation has a witty reply for everything. I do need to question her sanity, though. She's leaving that final thread up to you—the accident-prone resident novice witch.

Chapter Sixteen

MONDAY MORNING HAD dawned with a beautiful horizon, a warm coastal breeze, and that silver lining Ms. Stella had been referring to on Saturday evening. Much to Leo's delight and my relief, she hadn't truly left anything up to me. She'd wrapped everything up tight with a sparkly silver bow.

Speaking of glitter, this fairy dust kiss isn't wearing off my fur. I can't go through life with a fairy lipstick stain on my paw. I look ridiculous. No wonder Ivan won't let me join in on his weekly poker games.

"Here you go, my boy. Here you go," Beetle exclaimed in delight, pouring some more catnip out of a tiny bag and onto Leo's pillow that was in the windowsill of the tea shop. "This special treat is straight from Central Asia."

A few things you should know about my part-time employee. One, he resembled the mad scientist from *Back to the Future*, white hair and all. Two, he had a habit of repeating his phrases over and over, probably from dealing with a lot of older people when he'd work on their taxes as a young man. Also, he loved cardigan sweaters with colorful bowties and just so happened to be dating my mother as of late.

I can't talk about that latter subject just yet.

My brain hadn't quite accepted it as fate.

Let's just bypass that subject altogether, shall we? Let's concen-

trate on my BFF's special talents, and that is discovering the best premium organic catnip across the entire world. He really is one of a kind, isn't he? Hey, I have an outstanding suggestion—let's give Beetle the sapphire ring and make him immortal!

No one was going to be immortal, thanks to the binding spell I'd cast on the sapphire ring. And I was pleased to announce that the spell had been generated without a hitch.

You're two for two, Raven. You take the wins, and I'll take the credit.

Leo had given the proper guidance, and things were finally looking up in the witchcraft area.

You're forgetting that the resident warlock had opened a small portal for the afterlife to slip through, thus allowing Caroline Abigail Whitley to sense that someone had trifled with her remains. It was a good thing Ivan had spotted the door and was there to escort her back. I, of course, laid all of the blame on Joey's garbage-filled claws. I have two checks in the win column. He's simply going to have to keep up.

Speaking of wins, it appeared that Ms. Stella had found a way to tuck a replica of the ring in the lining of Caroline Abigail Whitley's dress that she'd been adorned in before her burial. Mr. Meyers had driven to the graveyard at Liam's request, and he'd discovered the miraculous find while conducting his responsibilities as a mortician—just as Ms. Stella had counted on.

Of course, Mr. Meyers had assumed that someone in his family had tried and failed to succeed in the family myth. He wasn't one to talk out of turn or seek attention, so he'd asked Liam not to make a record of the incident in any criminal reports.

Just as the Mistress of Manipulation had predicted. She truly is amazing. I mean, not as miraculous as my BFF and his ability to discover the most delicious herb in existence, but a close second. This Central Asian stuff is the bomb!

"My dear, Raven. Your mother took me to the most fabulous restaurant in New York City. Just fabulous," Beetle said, beaming to the point that I was pretty sure his white hair had a glow to the ends that were sticking straight up toward the ceiling. "The food was absolutely delicious, I tell you! Delicious beyond imagination!"

Speaking of delicious, this premium organic catnip from Central Asia might just top the minty herb from Honduras. I'll let you know when my tongue is no longer numb.

"I'm glad you had a good time in the city this weekend, Beetle." I poured both myself and Beetle a cup of coffee from the carafe I'd made before flipping over the open sign, careful not to mention my mother. As Leo and I had both agreed upon, it was a subject that needed to be avoided until we'd had more time to adjust to the odd relationship. "I also appreciate you coming in early this morning. Bree requested that tea blend I'd mixed by hand for the Mother's Day special we ran a couple of weeks ago, and it will take me a few hours to create the combination of tea leaves."

Raven, my tongue is still numb. Should it still be numb? Uh-oh. It's traveling. I can't feel my whiskers.

"Glad to be of help, my dear. Glad to be of help." Beetle was still standing in front of the windowsill with his hands on his hips. He did that a lot while waiting for customers and always announced when the bell was about to jingle above the door. "Liam's headed this way. It looks as if he's bringing you flowers."

I ate it all. Every leaf. I don't know how I did that without feeling my tongue. Sweet angel of mercy, what if I've swallowed my tongue?

I couldn't help but smile at the new tradition Liam started ever since I'd incorporated coffee into the shop's inventory. I still hadn't changed the name of the store, and I'd made the decision not to in honor of my Nan. She'd chosen the name *Tea, Leaves, & Eves*...and it should stay that way.

Seriously? I might have swallowed my tongue, and all you're thinking about is the name of the tea shop? Get your priorities straight, Raven!

As for Liam, he'd gotten into the habit of sneaking me coffee during the day. You see, I'd always thought it wouldn't be good for the tea shop if people believed I didn't prefer the beverage I was selling. I should mention that there were quite a few tea flavors that I really did enjoy, and now I had the best of both worlds. We had various coffee grinds and numerous tea blends, each as unique as our own Paramour Bay.

It's over for me. Did you hear me, Raven? Over. With no tongue, how am I ever going to ingest catnip again?

Now that Liam no longer had to sneak me coffee, he'd begun to bring me flowers every Monday. The fact that he remembered every week showed me just how lucky I was to have him in my life.

"Oh, I forgot to tell you how nice it was to get to know your Aunt Rowena over dinner," Beetle exclaimed, taking me by surprise so much that my gaze slid from Liam still crossing the street with a colorful bouquet of flowers. I must have been mistaken, because my mother and our Aunt Rowena avoided each other like the plague. "Such a nice woman, isn't she?"

Now I'm hearing things, Raven. Make it stop!

"Beetle, what do you mean you got to know Aunt Rowena better over dinner?" I asked cautiously, trying to brace myself for his answer.

An impossible feat. Maybe my BFF got a whiff of the Central Asia premium organic catnip and he's hallucinating. Dr. Jameson has to be wrong about overdosing on this delicious treat, because the world would have to be coming to an end before your mother would spend time with that witchery, witchy, witch of the West.

"Why, your Aunt Rowena was visiting your mother this weekend," Beetle shared, turning to give a wave to Liam as he approached the glass door of the tea shop. I did my best to return his smile, but I'm pretty sure I failed in that endeavor. "Look at those flowers, my dear. Look at them!"

I was too busy locking my gaze with Leo's, whose pupils were practically completely dilated from ingesting the special brand of premium organic catnip. There was only one reason why such a visit would occur—Aunt Rowena had been successful in recruiting my mother for the upcoming war with the coven.

This is it, Raven. The world really is ending. There's only one thing left to do—run for your life!

~ THE END ~

Thank you so much for reading Cryptic Blend! There are more comical shenanigans and magical chaos coming up in Broomstick Blend…

kennedylayne.com/broomstick-blend.html

A baffling whodunit arises while comical antics abound as USA Today Bestselling Author Kennedy Layne continues her Paramour Bay Mysteries…

Lady bugs, bumblebees, and butterflies are enjoying the humid summer days and nights in the quaint Connecticut coastal town of Paramour Bay. Completely exhausted, Raven Marigold is doing everything she can to keep her cool after the town mysteriously loses power. No electricity means no coffee…no coffee means that Raven's nerves are more than a bit frayed.

After a bit of investigating, Raven discovers evidence that witchcraft might have been involved in causing the power outage that has puzzled the residents and left them a little bit cranky. Well, their irritability turns into straight up panic when a possible murder victim is discovered smack dab in the middle of the town's cobblestone square.

Bring a flashlight if you want to help Raven and the rest of the gang solve this latest blackout mystery that will have you scrambling to turn the pages until the very last sentence!

ABOUT THE AUTHOR

First and foremost, I love life. I love that I'm a wife, mother, daughter, sister… and a writer.

I am one of the lucky women in this world who gets to do what makes them happy. As long as I have a cup of coffee (maybe two or three) and my laptop, the stories evolve themselves and I try to do them justice. I draw my inspiration from a retired Marine Master Sergeant that swept me off of my feet and has drawn me into a world that fulfills all of my deepest and darkest desires. Erotic romance, military men, intrigue, with a little bit of kinky chili pepper (his recipe), fill my head and there is nothing more satisfying than making the hero and heroine fulfill their destinies.

Thank you for having joined me on their journeys…

Email: kennedylayneauthor@gmail.com

Facebook: facebook.com/kennedy.layne.94

Twitter: twitter.com/KennedyL_Author

Website: www.kennedylayne.com

Newsletter: www.kennedylayne.com/aboutnewsletter.html